The **MYSTERY** of
Briar Rose Manor

Doris Davis

RadiantBOOKS

Gospel Publishing House/Springfield, Mo. 65802

02–0652

To Loren
Within his love I have found
Where I belong

Library of Congress Catalog Card Number 89–82583
International Standard Book Number 0–88243–652–x
Printed in the United States of America

Contents

1

Saying Good-bye

Janna fled through the darkness from an enemy whose face she couldn't see. She was weak and cold with fear. As she ran, her heart thudded until the blood roared in her ears. Sometimes she stumbled and almost fell. Each time, as she struggled to regain her balance, she knew that he was nearer. She ran on and on, gasping for air.

Then she was falling. Her arms flailed as she tried to grasp something to cling to. When she hit the bottom, she realized she was locked in a cage, still in darkness. The walls were closing around her, stifling her, smothering her. She fought to breathe.

With horror she realized that someone was in the cage with her. She could hear him moving slowly toward her in the darkness. Step by slow step he came. She felt him reach for her. She screamed in terror—and awoke.

Suddenly, her mother was there, smoothing her hair, talking quietly. Janna clung to her. Finally her heart stopped racing enough so that she was able to speak. She was still trembling.

"It was awful. I was locked in a cage and it was dark; someone evil was there with me." She shuddered.

"You haven't had a dream like that for years." Her

mother was shaking her head. "I'm sorry that Patty . . . What's-Her-Name locked you in a closet. I think her mother should have—no, that's not true. She was only five, just like you."

"But that's been so long ago—ten years," said Janna releasing her mother from her embrace. "I thought I was over the dreams. I haven't had one since I was about twelve. But," she admitted, "I'd still rather climb two hundred steps than ride two floors in an elevator. If I were ever alone in one and the light went out, I think I would die of fright."

"Remember what I would tell you after you had a dream like this?" Mother asked softly.

"I know, Mother, but my mind doesn't work too well when I'm scared. The verses just don't seem to come."

"Would you like to say one with me?"

"Sure."

" 'Even though I walk through the valley of the shadow of death, I will fear no evil, for you are with me'—Psalm 23:4. 'I will lie down and sleep in peace, for you alone, O Lord, make me dwell in safety'— Psalm 4:8."

Janna snuggled down in the covers. Even though she was a teenager, it did feel good to be babied once in a while. She felt safe and secure with her mother beside her.

"Do you want me to leave your door open?"

"Yes." The faint glow of a night-light lit the hall. It was enough: She drifted off into a dreamless sleep.

The next morning, Saturday, Janna woke up refreshed and excited. Memory of the nightmare had been pushed out of her mind—today was packing day! Tomorrow she would be taking the trip she had

6

been waiting for all year, the trip that would take her to meet her great aunt.

"How's the packing going?" her mother asked sometime later, poking her head in the doorway.

"I just don't think two suitcases will hold everything. This will be my third try," wailed Janna as she dumped the contents of a large blue suitcase on her bed: jogging shoes, swimsuit, tennis racket, camera, diary, stationery, and clothes.

Her mother smiled. "May I help?"

"Be my guest," Janna said as she flopped on the bed beside the suitcase. She ran her hands through her short, blonde hair, shook it vigorously, and then pushed her glasses up on her nose.

"I doubt if you'll need all these things. After all, Aunt Agatha is seventy-five years old. At that age she's not likely to want to play tennis."

"I'm sure someone there will. What's a vacation without tennis? And Briar Rose Manor is the kind of place that couldn't be without a swimming pool."

"The picture of Briar Rose Manor your aunt sent you is dated 1925. It may have changed."

"Not that much," Janna responded dreamily. Suddenly she bounced off the bed and picked up the photograph of the manor. What were the possibilities at Briar Rose Manor? Swimming? Tennis? Sunbathing? Meeting guys? Hmmm. She hadn't thought too much about guys, but that would top her vacation off just right.

"Don't set your hopes too high," Mother said. "Just enjoy whatever you find there."

"I still can't believe I'm actually going to meet Aunt Agatha." Janna turned to face her mother. "I wonder if she looks like her picture." Janna picked up the other photograph on her dresser and looked at the blonde-haired woman in it.

"I would guess that that picture was made at least thirty years ago," Mother said, looking up from organizing the pile on the bed for Janna's suitcase. "She looked older than that when I saw her at the funeral."

The funeral had been for Janna's real parents, who had been killed in an automobile accident. Janna was only six months old and had miraculously escaped injury. Aunt Agatha Louise Mitchell was the only relative who attended the funeral. The only relative Janna had, as a matter of fact.

Bill and Marsha Edmundson, good friends of her parents, had adopted her. Sometimes Janna wondered if they regretted their generosity. Especially since Kerri was born four years later, and Claude four years after that, and Baby Lisa only a year ago.

Janna put the picture back on the dresser as her mother smoothed the wrinkle on the bed where Janna had been sitting.

"I guess it's natural that you would want to meet your aunt, but don't forget that we're your family. We love you, and we need you."

"I love you, too," Janna said, hugging her mother.

The Edmundsons were so good to her. But for a year now she had felt out of place with them.

She looked at Marsha Edmundson with love, admiration, and envy: She was small, dark-haired, and lovely; her every movement graceful. Beside her, Janna felt as awkward and gawky as a giraffe—all sharp elbows and knobby knees. She was already two inches taller than her adoptive mother, and still growing. Her dresses always looked as if their hems needed to be let out. And most of her long-sleeved blouses couldn't be buttoned at the cuff. Janna's blonde hair and fair skin contrasted with her mother's dark complexion. No one would mistake Marsha Edmundson and Janna for mother and daughter by their looks, that was certain.

Why couldn't I have at least been pretty? Janna thought as she watched her mother finish packing the suitcases.

"Be sure to hang your dresses in the closet as soon as you can at Aunt Agatha's," her mother said as she folded the green dress that her dad especially liked. He said that it turned her eyes green. If she had one good feature, Janna decided, it was her eyes. But she was as nearsighted as Mr. McGoo and had to wear glasses, which she felt hid them. So why didn't she take her folks up on their offer to get her contacts? Maybe she wanted to hide . . .

"Thanks for packing for me. I could never get all that stuff in there and make it look so neat."

"You have virtues, sweetheart, that are just as important as neatness. You have the ability to plan and organize things, like the youth outings at church. That's something I'd rather not tackle."

Mother often tried to point out Janna's strengths. But Janna always felt she was just saying nice things.

No matter how hard Janna tried, she just couldn't be neat. Not that neatness mattered much to her. She just saw it as another difference between her and the Edmundsons. They were all naturally neat: Kerri, Claude, even Baby Lisa. Their rooms always looked like pictures from *Better Homes and Gardens* while hers usually resembled a bargain basement after a twelve-hour sale.

Lisa toddled into the room pulling a waggle-tailed toy dog. She had just learned to walk. The joy she felt in this accomplishment showed in a white-toothed smile. As she entered the room she toppled over. She sat up and grinned at Janna. Janna scooped her up and lifted her high over her head. Lisa laughed, and Janna brought her down to cuddle her. She put her mouth on the baby's neck and blew. Lisa giggled.

If only you were my real little sister, Janna thought as she looked into Lisa's dark brown eyes.

Janna knew that she wasn't the only one who felt that she wasn't a true Edmundson. She felt out of place at family reunions. To make matters worse, there was that family tree that Dad's sister was working on. Kerri was on it, and Claude, and Lisa. But it didn't have a twig on it for her.

Other people noticed the differences, too. Janna grew hot as she remembered the rude comment made by Kate Flannery at the church picnic. All of the Edmundsons stood in a group as they got plates from their picnic basket. Kate stared at the family for a moment and then exclaimed to Janna, "You certainly are the oddball of the family."

Janna was ready to jump Kate, when her mother spoke up, "That's the beautiful thing about family—you belong because you *are* family, not because you're like your family." Janna's anger dissolved in a mixture of gratitude and amusement. Gratitude for her mother's defense as well as for her witness—Kate was not a Christian. Amusement because the flush on her mother's face betrayed her own struggle to hold herself under control—calm, self-contained Mother, who had been working with Janna in controlling her own temper! Even so, Kate Flannery was right. No matter how much Janna ached to belong, she just didn't.

But now Janna realized she had Aunt Agatha. She

10

and Aunt Agatha shared a blood tie. She just knew that she would feel a spiritual bond with Aunt Agatha that would be different from any she had ever felt for anyone else. It would be an attraction that would have drawn them together even if they had met as strangers, unaware of their relationship. A kinship. A mystical tie.

Janna longed for the meeting. She knew that then she would finally experience the wholeness she had hungered for as she grew to understand that she was adopted and had no natural family.

Even though Janna had been wanting to visit Aunt Agatha for the past few summers, her parents felt she wasn't old enough to make the day-long bus trip alone. Finally her parents felt it would be all right for her to travel this summer, especially since her best friend, Brooke, would be traveling with her as far as Carlisle to visit her married sister. Janna would spend the night and resume her trip early the next afternoon.

Sunday brought the usual activities with a touch of specialness. Janna's Sunday school class said good-bye and her mother prepared a going-away dinner for both Janna and Brooke.

"Everybody to Janna's room," said her dad. "We'll clear her out in one move." He gave Janna a wink.

The whole family piled in the car to see them off at the station. Dad turned around in his seat.

"Everybody in?" he asked. "Since this will be the last time we'll all be together in a quiet place before Janna leaves, let's pray for Brooke and Janna on their trip. Any volunteers?"

"Dad, I'd like you to pray," Janna said. She always felt strength and comfort when her father prayed, especially if it was specifically for her.

11

"Okay. . . . Heavenly Father," he began, "we thank You for our friends and our families. We know You have placed each of us in our families to make us all complete. We ask for Your protection of Brooke and Janna while they are apart from us. May Brooke's time with her sister be special and may Janna's time with Aunt Agatha help her to understand better who she is as Your special child. Amen."

Claude sat close to Janna. He took her hand and held it all the way to the bus station.

When the car stopped, Janna leaned over and said to him, "Did you know you're my favorite brother?"

"I am?" He looked up at her with big eyes.

Janna nodded.

Claude was silent for a moment, and then burst out, "Hey! I'm your *only* brother."

"And still my favorite." Janna hugged him. "Don't you forget it."

Dad checked her suitcases in, and Mother and the children surrounded Janna. All during the ride to the bus station, eleven-year-old Kerri had tried to hide a brown paper sack. Now she opened it. She drew out a small box that was tied with a green ribbon. She handed it to Janna.

"It's a going-away present. Open it."

Janna tore off the wrapping. The box held a pair of barrettes. Janna smiled and bent to hug her sister.

"Thank you. When I wear them, I'll think of you."

Lisa leaned from her mother's arms toward Janna. When Janna took her, the baby covered her face with wet kisses. Even she seemed to understand that Janna would be away for a while.

Mother hugged her and said softly, "We'll be loving you and praying for you while you're gone, honey."

"Thanks, Mom," Janna replied with tears in her

12

eyes. Good-byes always made Janna realize how much she loved this family.

Janna looked at each family member. *I'll hide this moment in my memory treasure chest and keep it forever and ever,* she thought.

After Brooke and Janna boarded the bus, Brooke said, "You sit next to the window so you can wave to them."

Janna's face lighted. She scooted into the seat and looked out on her family. They stood near the bus, faces upturned as they tried to make her out behind the dark glass.

She tapped on the window with her knuckles. Her father's eyes found her first. He pointed toward her window. She could almost hear him say, "There she is!" For a minute kisses were thrown and waves exchanged between Janna and the small cluster of people below.

As the bus started to pull out, Janna waved one last time and then sank back in her seat. Tears filled her eyes.

Brooke looked at Janna with curiosity. "Why are you crying? You'll be back before you know it."

Janna wiped her eyes and took a deep breath.

"I haven't told anyone, but since you're my best friend, I want to tell you. I probably won't be living with them any more."

Brooke's eyes got big. Then she leaned toward Janna. "Why? Have you got some strange, incurable disease you haven't told me about?"

Although Janna smiled, her words sobered Brooke. "No. But Aunt Agatha and I belong together. We've been writing to each other for years. I know she'll ask me to live with her, and of course I'll have to say yes. After all, we're blood relatives. . . . Only I do love Mom and Dad and Kerri and Claude and Lisa so. I'll miss them."

Brooke was quiet for a moment. "It will be hard to leave them. And I will really miss you. You're the best friend I have. But you have to do what you have to do." Her voice was dramatic. Then her face brightened. "You'll probably just love living at Briar Rose Manor. Even the name gives me goose bumps. I can just see the sparkling chandeliers and the graceful, curving stairway. Let me see the picture again."

Janna searched in her bag, then brought out a brown envelope. From it she drew a photograph: an impressive house surrounded by beautifully landscaped grounds. Carefully, almost reverently, she gave it to Brooke.

"It's so lovely," sighed Brooke. "I almost wish I could trade places with you. You'll probably have servants and go to Europe every summer."

"Oooh, that would be fun," Janna said. "But that's not what I want most. I just want to be with my really, truly relative. I want her to tell me about my family. You can't imagine what it's like not to know who you really are."

Brooke thought for a moment. "It would be like if you were a sailboat drifting alone on the ocean—not knowing where you came from or where you're going."

Janna sighed. It was so comforting to have a friend who understood.

"Or it's as if you were told to paint a picture and you looked at the palette of colors and there was no yellow. Something vital is missing in your life."

Janna nodded.

"It's like you're on a stage and you're waiting for your cue—and there is none."

Janna blinked. Her friend was getting warmed up.

14

"It's like—"

"Brooke, you know your roots, don't you?"

"Oh, yeah, sure," said Brooke without a pause. "I know all four of my grandparents and we can trace our family back to 1623. I have scads of relatives and ancestors."

"All I have is Aunt Agatha. You can understand why I'll go live with her when she asks me to."

Brooke nodded. "I'll miss you."

"I'll miss you, too," Janna said.

"Hey!" Brooke said. "Maybe your aunt will have a family tree."

The girls continued to talk. Every once in a while the bus would stop at a station. Some people got off; others got on. After a while the bus driver announced, "We'll be stopping in Edensdale for ten minutes."

"I'm beginning to get hungry. I want to get some potato chips and a Coke," Brooke said.

"But we don't want to spoil our appetites for your sister's supper."

"Oh, I won't. I get hungrier when I'm excited. And I'm pretty excited!"

"Well, okay, but let's hurry so the bus won't leave without us. I don't want to get stranded," said Janna as the bus slowed to a stop.

Later, when the bus driver announced Carlisle, the two girls collected their things and prepared to leave. As the bus pulled into the station, Brooke leaned across Janna to look out the window in search of her sister.

"There's Donna! And little Don! I can't wait to hold him." She looked at Janna. "Let's go."

But Janna hung back and watched wistfully as the sisters—blood sisters—hugged each other. And

15

the night in Carlisle passed so quickly that Janna was saying good-bye to Brooke for the summer before either of them realized it.

"Be sure to remember everything that happens so you can tell me about it," said Brooke, who had accompanied Janna onto the bus. Then she was hurrying through the aisle and down the steps. Joining her sister and nephew, Brooke turned to wave good-bye. Slowly the bus pulled out of the station and Janna's journey was resumed.

Janna's new seatmate was a thin, dark-haired woman in a rumpled brown pantsuit. As Janna settled in, her seatmate asked with mild curiosity, "Where are you going?"

"Mineville, Missouri, to visit my aunt."

But the woman had been traveling for two days already and was no longer interested in conversation. For the next hours she alternately read and dozed. Janna didn't mind. She had much to think about. Her thoughts turned first to the home she had left in Cincinnati. What was the family doing now? Did anyone miss her yet? Were they glad to have her gone for a while so they could be together as a natural family?

Then her mind reached ahead to her journey's end. *Since Aunt Agatha doesn't have a car she won't be able to meet me at the station,* she thought. But she had her aunt's directions to the manor so she planned to take a cab.

When I get out of the cab tonight, Aunt Agatha will come hurrying to me. When she hugs me I'll pretend that she's my grandmother. Or even my real mother!

A tingle of anticipation ran through Janna. Her cheeks were pink and her eyes sparkled.

16

Aunt Agatha would lead Janna into Briar Rose Manor and everything would proclaim its owner's happiness at her coming. Furniture would be polished to a mirror-bright sheen. Freshly cut roses would have been placed throughout the rooms. Wafting from the kitchen would be the aroma of something delicious cooking for dinner. Best of all would be the love in Aunt Agatha's shining eyes and warm smile.

I wonder how long it will take Aunt Agatha to ask me to live with her.

Janna's thoughts were so busy that the miles passed quickly for a while. As she stared out the window, she wished Brooke had stayed on the bus with her; the time passed much faster when she had someone to talk to. She was tired of thinking so much. And she still had hours to ride. Finally she found a half-way comfortable position and fell asleep.

As Janna slept on the bus, the early-rising moon drew an angular old house from the darkness miles away. In the front yard the age-whitened skeletons of two dead sycamore trees stood guard. Untrimmed roses climbed the walls of the house and reached across the windows as if to conceal secrets within.

Upper story windows gave an occasional glimmer of light—until one by one their blinds were tightly pulled. The light from the rising moon disturbed the purpose of the one who carried the small, but powerful flashlight.

As the moon rose higher it revealed the name on the mailbox just outside the thorny hedge that half hid the house from the road: A. L. Mitchell.

2

Briar Rose Manor

Mineville, Missouri, was a small town. The bus rolled down an almost empty Main Street. In Cincinnati, the city would be just coming alive.

Large clouds moved slowly overhead. Trying to sustain the twilight, the corner streetlights succeeded only in encircling themselves with a florescent glow. A grocery store and the filling station that served as the bus stop were lighted; a few people sauntered in and out through their open doors. All other businesses were closed for the day.

As the bus came to a stop, Janna felt relieved that her trip had finally come to an end. It had passed uneventfully. She had dozed off and on all day in between the frequent stops, now and then going into the "care package" Brooke's sister had sent with Janna and finally making a meal of it for supper.

It seemed like ages ago—rather than the evening before—that she had said good-bye to the Edmundsons. She needed to stretch and was looking forward to a good night's sleep. But her heart quickened as she got up, and her mouth was dry with excitement. She had waited a long time to meet her only living relative.

Janna showed her luggage receipts to the bus driver and claimed her suitcases. Then she looked around for a cab. One was parked at the curb and the driver was at the wheel. Janna hurried over to the driver, who was moving and rubbing his eyes as if he had just been awakened (which he had).

"Can you take me out into the country?" she asked. "I have the directions." She handed him the page from her aunt's letter.

The driver had a bulge in his cheek that Janna thought was some kind of tumor. Squinting up at her, he said, "Looks to be a few miles."

"This was the closest bus stop to my aunt's house." Janna knew it would be a ways from Mineville, but her father had given her enough fare for a taxi.

"Who's your aunt?" he asked as he slowly got out of the car.

"Miss Agatha Mitchell," Janna replied.

He stretched. "The ol' Mitchell place, then." He rubbed the stubble on his chin as he cocked his head and squinted at her again. "Not many people go out thataway." His voice got lower. "Lot a strange tales about the ol' place."

Janna was excited at being so near the end of her journey and so impatient with the slowness of the cab driver that she paid no attention to his words. Cincinnati drivers didn't take time to talk to their riders. And she didn't like the way he had looked at her.

The man shifted the "tumor" in his mouth and spit a stream of brown liquid. *Yuk!* thought Janna, trying not to looked shocked. *It's tobacco. This is definitely not Cincinnati.* She looked around for another cab, but didn't see one.

Janna watched as the driver loaded her suitcases. Then turning to her he said, "You can ride in the front seat if you're of a mind to."

19

"No, thank you," said Janna as she got in the back seat opposite the driver's seat.

"Suit yourself," said the driver as he spit another stream and ambled to his door. Just as he settled himself in, a boy came loping up.

"Ned, I need a ride out to my place. How much?"

The boy, a year or two older than Janna, was tall; as he looked down at the driver, a slow grin spread over the boy's freckled face.

Suddenly the driver seemed to be on the defensive. "Now Mike, you know what it is. I gotta have three dollars."

"Two dollars is all I've got on me." Janna noticed that his voice cracked slightly. But he was still grinning.

"Now I cain't do it for no two dollars."

"Ned," the boy lowered his voice. "I saw you load another passenger. Where you goin'?"

"Aw, Mike, that don't make no difference. You pay for you. She pays for her." The driver had lowered his voice too. Janna was forgetting her anxiety and frustration about the driver and trying, from her position in the back seat, to see more than the infectious grin of the speaker.

"Quart of goat's milk and two dollars," said Mike.

"I don't even like goat's milk—like drinking the smell of a goat."

"But you're wife likes it."

"How do you know that!"

"Ned, I know everybody who likes my product and those who might be persuaded."

"Dadburned woman—get in!"

"Great!" He opened the car door and climbed into the back seat. Janna looked at him without trying to stare. Cute, for sure. Probably a basketball player, with that height. His knees came up sharply behind the driver's seat.

So Missouri does have good-looking guys, Janna thought as she pushed her glasses up on her nose.

The boy turned to her and smiled, nodding a shock of red hair. "Hey," he said. "My name's Mike ... Mike Morris."

Despite the odd greeting, Janna's heart did a flip-flop. That grin did something to you.

"Hi, my name's Janna Edmundson."

"You're new around here, aren't you?"

"I came to visit my aunt at Briar Rose Manor."

He looked blank. "Never heard of it. Is that some kind of country club?"

"It's my aunt's estate. Miss Agatha Mitchell is my aunt."

"Oh, the Mitchell place. Sure, I know it. I pass it every day."

"You do?"

"On my milk route."

"Oh."

He was rubbing his hands on his knees. "Ned, can we hear some music?"

The driver turned on the radio, hit the dash a couple of times, and someone sang about the milk of love gone sour.

Mike leaned toward Janna and said, "Look, I hope you didn't think I was taking advantage of Ned. That's just kinda the way I go at payin' for things that don't have a set price."

Ummm, what is that cologne he's wearing? She smiled, thinking that guys in Cincinnati usually worked at a place like McDonald's for a part-time job.

"How many goats do you have?"

"I milk six. Besides the nannies, I have eight kids and a billy."

Whatever that means, thought Janna. "Does my aunt take your milk?"

"No," he answered slowly and then grinned. "Do you like goat's milk?"

Janna laughed . . .

The road was winding and hilly; with the aid of the full moon when it was not hidden by clouds, Janna could make out grazing cattle in the fenced pastures on both sides of the road. Patches of woodland broke the monotony of open fields.

"I get out here," the boy said suddenly. "Ned, I can run get that quart now or drop it off later."

"It don't make me no difference if I never see that stuff," said the driver as he pulled to a stop.

"Now a deal's a deal, Ned. I'll just drop it by later," said Mike with a chuckle. "Nice to meet you, Janna."

"Bye," Janna said, suppressing a giggle.

The driver hit the dash, although the radio seemed to be playing clearly, and resumed speed.

Mike Morris, Janna repeated. She would have to remember that name. *He's a little different from the boys back home, but he might make a good tennis partner. I'll have to ask Aunt Agatha about him.* She made a mental note to do that tomorrow.

Twilight had given way to darkness, and when the clouds covered the moon, the darkness was total: no illuminated intersections, no street lights, only an isolated pole light now and then between a barn and a house. The cab turned off the main road onto a dirt road. It seemed dreamlike to be hurtling through the night with only the beams of the headlights offering any illumination. They had passed neither car nor lighted house since leaving the pavement.

It will be good to be in a brightly lighted house,
Janna thought. She decided that twilight in the
country was a lonesome time, even eerie. She shivered. As long as she could remember, she had been
afraid of the dark. In Cincinnati, streetlights brightened every block. Even at night there were people
on the streets and the noise of traffic was constant.

"Doesn't anyone live on this road?" asked Janna.

"Not many. Cain't make a living on a little farm
no more. Most of the small farmers have sold out
and moved into town. Lots of old houses standing
empty out here."

"Empty houses are sad," she said. *And scary,* she
added to herself.

The cab slowed and the driver stopped before a
hedge fronting a tall, gaunt house half hidden by
trees and overgrown shrubbery. The driver opened
his door and a dome light fought weakly against the
darkness in the cab.

Janna looked apprehensively at the dark house.
The blinds on both the upper and lower story windows were pulled. She could almost hear the house
speaking, *There are deep secrets hidden under my
roof. Only those who belong here are welcome.*

"There must be some mistake," Janna said. "Are
you sure that this is where Agatha Mitchell lives?"

"Yep."

"Mother was right. It has changed since 1925,"
Janna mumbled to herself. "And not in a way I like."

Janna crawled out of the cab and paid the driver.
He looked through the darkness at the shadowed
house.

"Don't look like nobody's home. Maybe you'll be
wanting to go back to town. Won't charge extra for

23

it. Motel there'll put you up for the night. Could come back tomorrow."

"Aunt Agatha is expecting me," Janna insisted. And as if to commend her decision, a full moon broke through the clouds. Janna took courage. "If she isn't here now, I'm sure she will be soon. Thanks for being concerned, but I'll be all right."

Shaking his head, the driver reached for her suitcases and carried them to the edge of the yard near a gate. He added more tobacco to the wad in his mouth and got back in his car.

Janna stood by the gate and watched as he turned the car in the road and retreated toward town. The taillights—*they look like cat's eyes,* thought Janna—might have hypnotized her if a hill hadn't finally hidden their stare. Janna blinked, then turned slowly toward the house. In the presence of the cab driver she had felt safe, but now that she was alone her courage faltered.

Strange that Aunt Agatha didn't have a light on. If it hadn't been for the full moon, Janna couldn't have made out the house. It was a two-story frame house, weathered by years of sun, wind, and rain. The house had aged gracelessly, without beauty, and had long ago relinquished any claim to style and grandeur. Any resemblance to the pictured mansion she had dreamed over was only structural. *The way it looks now, the Jaycees could turn it into a good haunted house,* thought Janna.

"Well, it's not exactly what I expected for my summer vacation," she murmured to herself sadly. "But at least I have real family here."

When Janna pushed open the sagging gate it squeaked dismally. Suddenly it grew dark; she looked up to see a thick cloud over the moon. A shudder ran

24

down her spine. She glanced warily around her, trying to penetrate the blackness. She picked up her two suitcases and trudged up the stone path to the front door. Weeds, knee-high, brushed against both suitcases as she walked.

Janna saw no signs of life. She crossed a creaking front porch, knocked timidly at the door, then waited. No one came.

At Janna's knock a person in the house froze at the top of the stairway. He clicked off the small flashlight he carried and stood in the darkness, waiting and listening.

Janna knocked again, harder. At age seventy-five Aunt Agatha was probably hard of hearing. Perhaps, too, she was in one of the back rooms, or upstairs. Janna pounded on the door. She wished that she hadn't sent the cab driver away so soon. If only Aunt Agatha would hurry.

Uneasily Janna stole a look behind her. She reassured herself that the dark shapes she noticed were simply untrimmed shrubbery—but was there a movement in the clump at the corner of the house?

In sudden unreasoning panic, Janna banged again on the door. The sound reverberated through the boards of the porch beneath her feet. She leaned her head against the door.

Maybe the cab driver was wrong. Maybe this was an abandoned old house . . . occupied only by ghosts, Janna thought. She shivered. Then she remembered seeing a mailbox beside the gate as she got out of the cab. Perhaps there was a name on it. She would check. Leaving her suitcases on the porch, she walked quickly back to the mailbox. She stooped to peer at the side. She pushed her glasses up higher on her nose, although she was nearsighted and she might as well have taken them off. The clouds played with the moon; she strained to decipher the weathered name. A. L. Mitchell. That would be Aunt Agatha, all right: Agatha Louise Mitchell.

Considering her reception, Janna couldn't decide if that was good news or bad news.

She turned back to the front porch. Strange that Aunt Agatha didn't seem to be at home. Janna hadn't expected to be met at the bus station, but her aunt had known that she was coming and had even seemed eager for the visit. She surely hadn't forgotten. Besides that, Aunt Agatha had written that she never went anywhere except on Sundays when she went to church and then got her groceries.

Janna stumbled over the rough path. On reaching the door, she knocked loudly again. When no one appeared, she tested the doorknob. The door was unlocked! What should she do? It didn't seem right to enter someone else's house. But she had been invited, she reminded herself. As she hesitated, a wild, blood-curdling scream split the air beside the house. For an eternity it hung quivering. Then silence.

Janna froze. Then she pushed the door open and, jumping inside, slammed it shut. As she leaned weakly against the door, she waited in terror for another scream. The only sounds were the pounding of her heart and the ticking of a clock.

There had been no movement from the person at the top of the stairs until Janna burst through the door. Then, silently as a specter, he stole back into one of the rooms and stepped into a closet.

3

Is Anybody Home?

Gradually Janna grew calm.

"Aunt Agatha?" she called. "It's me, Janna."

She heard nothing.

She tried to see into the room where she stood. *The blinds on the windows work well,* Janna thought. *I might as well be blind. . . . Well, the blind see with their hands. I can too.*

The light switch should be by the door. She slid her hands over the wall along both sides of the door. Then she remembered: Aunt Agatha had written that she didn't have electricity. When she had read that, it sounded like fun to live as simply as the pioneers had lived, but now an electric light would certainly be welcome. She was beginning to wonder how she had kept the country club idea of Briar Rose Manor alive.

Turning to her left as she faced the door, Janna cautiously put one hand out in front of her and touched the wall with the other one as she moved. She moved away from the door and followed the wall for a short distance, coming to an inside corner. She followed the new wall for an equally short distance and came to a doorway. She paused.

Think, Janna! Think, she said to herself. "But I can't," she answered her thoughts aloud. She took a deep breath. *Now I lay me down to sleep. . . .* "The Lord is my shepherd. I shall not want . . . to run. He makes me to lie down in green pastures. He leads me beside . . . hall walls"—it was a guess about the arrangement of the house, but it made sense. You just didn't come in off a porch into someone's bedroom or bathroom. She congratulated herself for being able to use her head at a time like this.

She decided to go through the doorway. Turning immediately to her right, she felt along the wall of the new room in the same fashion as before. She went a short distance and was back at the outside wall of the house. *Wall number one,* she decided. She had gone a few steps when the wall seemed to give. Feeling a little farther she realized this was a window and she was feeling a canvas-like curtain. She lifted one edge and could make out the porch, but she was uncertain about how to raise the curtain. She let it drop back into position, which made it darker for her eyes.

"Ouch!" She had bumped into a wooden box. She bent to rub her shin. She'd have a purple bruise there. She felt guardedly over the top of the knee-high box. It held sticks of wood. Was there a fireplace close by?

She moved on. Another inside corner. "This is the second wall," she said to herself. She realized she had begun talking to herself. "I wonder how healthy that is. Oh well, maybe it will help me keep my sanity. That sounds healthy."

About waist high, her hands touched something smooth and hard and cold. Something metal. *A stove of some kind,* she thought. *An antique wood stove, I bet, just like Dad would go for. That explains the wood box,* she thought triumphantly. A shelf next to the stove held several containers of various sizes. She continued on. Her hands slid over a closed door, curtained like the window, and then she was at another inside corner.

Turning the corner she took a few steps and collided with a tall piece of furniture. She fumbled on around it. This was the third wall, she told herself. She soon should reach her starting point.

Oh, good, the corner, she thought.

She felt a small table with some items on it that she couldn't identify, and beyond that—the open doorway. After savoring the accomplishment of having found four walls of a room, she wondered what was out in the middle of the floor.

She reached toward the center of the room. Her fingers touched a chair. Table and chairs—of course, she was in the kitchen. Carefully her hands explored the tabletop. A candle in a holder! Janna's hands flew over the table again in a search for matches. Besides the candle, the table held only a fruit bowl.

Where in a kitchen would matches be kept? "Near the stove," she answered. "Maybe this talking to myself isn't so bad. At least I'm coming up with some answers." She laughed nervously at herself.

She remembered a small metal container on the shelf near the stove. It had rattled when she shook it. She found it again and took off the cover. She felt inside. Stick matches! Eagerly she struck one on the rusty bottom of the box. The smell of sulphur rose from the match, then a yellow flame flared. Janna reached for the candle. Soon its flickering light sent shadows dancing eerily over the walls. Janna surveyed the room. Unframed pictures were tacked on the walls, calendar pictures collected over the years apparently.

An apron hung on a peg on the wall. There was a small table that held a wash pan and a water bucket.

Although the room was neat and orderly, the few pieces of old furniture made it look deserted and unused.

Suddenly Janna remembered that she had left her luggage outside. But what about that scream? She felt her skin prickle at the memory, and the hair on the back of her neck stiffened.

"I wonder if I can survive without my stuff until morning," she said out loud.

"Oh, don't be such a baby," she answered herself. "Act like a fifteen-year-old and bring in your suitcases."

Carrying the candle with her, she walked slowly into the hall. Immediately to her right she noticed stairs going up to the second floor; the candle cast its light only halfway up.

But her mission was her luggage. After placing the candle on a small shelf in the hall, she approached the door. She stood there for a moment with her hand on the knob. Then she tore open the door and darted out. Jerking up a suitcase in each hand, she practically flew back inside the house. She dropped the suitcases and slammed the door. Leaning against the wall, her heart throbbing wildly against her ribs like a bird beating against the bars of its cage, she watched the candle dancing with the disturbance of the air in the hall, almost going out.

"No!" she whispered fiercely and held her breath. *Great,* she thought. *Not only am I talking to myself, I'm now talking to candles.*

When the flame stopped fluttering, she noted with relief that the door had a lock that didn't need a key. At least this entrance was safe. And next to the door leaned a walking stick. *It could serve as a kind of club,* thought Janna. She picked it up; she felt safer with it in her hand.

But where could Aunt Agatha be? Perhaps she had fallen somewhere in the house and needed help. Janna picked up the candle and walked down the long shadowy hall, trying to ignore the stairs.

"Aunt Agatha," she called in a trembling voice.

Janna felt that she had never experienced such silence. In the city there were lights and people— and noise. All the tumult of the city blended to make a constant roar. Here there were sounds, but each was separate. The sputtering candle and, some- where, a ticking clock seemed only to add to the sense of quiet. Janna had never felt so alone.

Then she saw the indistinct figure at the far end of the hall. It also carried a flickering candle.

"Aunt Agatha!" she cried, walking as quickly down the hall as the candle would allow. The figure hur- ried to meet her.

But something was wrong. Janna slowed down and looked at the figure. She realized that she was mov- ing toward her own reflection. It was mirrored in the glass of a door at the end of the hall. She was still alone.

Janna shivered uncontrollably. If only her father were here the house wouldn't seem hostile. She re- membered the strength she had felt when he prayed for her before she left home. If he were here, the shadows would settle down and his voice would fill the frightening stillness. She could almost hear him reminding her, *Jesus is always with you.* Though this thought was of comfort, Janna longed for some- one she could touch.

Still, she must continue her search. She went back

31

to the front of the house and looked up the stairs. It was dark and foreboding. She decided to check all the downstairs rooms for her aunt. She was probably sound asleep somewhere in the house.

To give her a free hand for opening doors, she decided to hang the cane on the wrist of the hand that carried the candle. She started with the door across from the kitchen. Slowly she opened the door, then took the cane in hand, and eased back the door. It led into a large carpeted parlor.

The furniture was sheet-covered except for a cot and a straight-backed kitchen chair. This was where the clock was. It was a grandfather clock, taller than Janna herself. Its pendulum reflected the light of the candle with each passing second.

The walls were covered with what must be family portraits. Staring grimly at her from across the room were oil paintings of an unsmiling bearded man and a grim-faced woman. The woman's hair was pulled back into a tight knot. Her great-great-grandparents? They seemed displeased at her intrusion.

She reentered the hall and closed the parlor door. Involuntarily she looked up the stairs. She tiptoed down the hall to the next door. Her inclination was to hurry; she wanted to escape whatever lurked in the shadows. But when she moved quickly, the candle flame threatened to go out. She found that the door to this room was locked.

She crossed the hall and opened the last door. Swiftly she scanned the room. No Aunt Agatha. This was a bedroom. Perhaps the one she would use. She closed the door and stood surveying the hall. The stairs near the front door drew her relentlessly.

A drop of hot wax touched Janna's hand. She glanced down at her candle. It had been short when she had lighted it. Now it was little more than a stub. How much longer would it burn? Even by candlelight the house was spooky; in darkness her first fears would return. Janna knew that she must hasten her search for Aunt Agatha before the light was gone.

She hurried upstairs. Every step squeaked. She found a hall with two closed doors on each side. She paused on the landing; the quivering candlelight struggled on the walls and ceiling with deep shadows. Behind a closet door, someone listened intently for Janna's movement. "Aunt Agatha?" She waited for an answer.

None came.

She tiptoed to the first room on the right and warily turned the knob. As she inched the door open, it creaked loudly. Chills went up and down Janna's back. Inside the closet a figure pressed against the wall. She held the candle high and examined the room. It contained boxes, old chairs, and stacks of magazines, a sort of storeroom, but no Aunt Agatha.

She crossed the hall. In this room so many faces stared down at her that it seemed the walls were papered with portraits. One huge painting of Briar Rose Manor in its prime dominated the picture gallery.

She crept down the hall and tried the door on her left. She breathed a sigh of relief at the familiar sight of a library. Shelves of books lined the walls. A massive desk, weighed down with a clutter of papers, was covered with a layer of dust.

But when Janna crossed the hall and opened the fourth door, her heart dropped and her mouth went dry. A sheet-covered figure lay motionless on a couch.

33

The palms of Janna's hands were cold and sweaty. Had she found Aunt Agatha?

Janna's knees were so weak that she thought she would drop to the floor. She crept toward the couch. What if Aunt Agatha were sick and unconscious? There was no telephone and apparently no close neighbor. What if she were dead? The figure on the couch had not moved since Janna first saw it. Her face was ashen and the candlelight shook with the tremor of her hands.

Candle in one hand and cane in the other, she reached the shrouded body. Using the cane she lifted back the sheet. The body had no head! Janna laughed hysterically. She had uncovered a dress form. Aunt Agatha must be a seamstress.

Janna replaced the cover and giggled nervously. "Sorry, Myrtle. Go back to sleep."

Janna had run out of rooms to try. Aunt Agatha didn't seem to be upstairs. Janna closed the door softly and walked toward the stairway. Halfway down she had an almost uncontrollable urge to run the rest of the way. She felt that eyes were watching her. With every ounce of will she possessed, she forced herself to stand still and look back up the staircase. She saw no one. She compelled herself to descend slowly to the last step.

Janna peered down the hallway. The only light in the house was the candle she carried, but the wavering shapes it created were unnerving. Her inclination was to return to the familiarity of the kitchen, close herself in, and sit with her back against the wall while she waited for daylight.

But Aunt Agatha might be unconscious in some part of the house she hadn't yet explored. She must go on. The only place she hadn't checked was the basement, if the old house had one. She had seen a door near the back of the house that she guessed would lead downstairs. She went to the door; it was locked . . . no, it appeared to be sealed.

She turned around to the back door, to check its security, and slid its bolt into place. At least she was now barricaded against the unknown terrors from without.

The candle was now little more than an odorous wick in a puddle of melted wax. She decided to give up her search and prepare for bed while she still had light. She was exhausted from the long trip and felt that even being in a scary house wouldn't keep her awake tonight.

She set the candle on the shelf in the hall. After taking her luggage to the bedroom she returned to the kitchen with the candle. It seemed like she had had no food for hours. In her purse were a candy bar and half a sandwich wrapped in a napkin, left over from what Brooke's sister had packed. Janna looked on the curtained set of shelves. There were dishes on one shelf, pans on another, and food on two others. She grabbed a solitary apple from the dish on the table and a package of crackers from a shelf and hurried back to the bedroom as quickly as the dying candle would permit.

Though the outside doors were secure, still Janna didn't feel safe. How could she fortify her room? There were no locks on her door. She propped a chair against the knob to hold the door shut. What about the windows? To her dismay she found that neither the window onto the side yard nor the one that looked out onto the back porch had a lock. She would have to rely on the hooked screen . . . which didn't look all that secure.

Don't be ridiculous, Janna told herself. *Just because you're in a strange place doesn't mean you'll be murdered in your bed. You searched the house and no one's here. Tomorrow you'll find why Aunt Agatha isn't here and you'll feel silly for being scared* . . . "But perhaps Aunt Agatha *is* here. There's one room you haven't searched," she was talking aloud to herself again. "The room across the hall, the one behind the locked door. What's in it?"

Just then the candle gave a last sputter and died. Janna groaned.

She collected her food and sat on the edge of the bed to eat it. Everything seemed strangely tasteless when she couldn't see.

She felt that the dreadful darkness was a dream. Reality was back in Cincinnati. . . . What was happening at home now? Probably Dad and Mother were alone in the living room. Mother would have heard the bedtime prayers of Kerri and Claude and would have kissed them and Lisa goodnight. She wondered if they had prayed for her. Dad said that each of them had a guardian angel. Never before had she felt that she needed one, but now she welcomed the thought. Janna was glad that her parents loved God.

Her parents? She felt a twinge of pain. *Not really my parents,* she told herself. She belonged to Aunt Agatha—and to the stern-faced couple in the parlor. But she couldn't find Aunt Agatha, and the man and the woman in the other room were no longer alive. They were only ghosts now. Ghosts! Janna could almost feel someone standing beside her bed.

She rolled the apple core and the candy wrapper in the paper towel, then she dropped them on the floor under the bed. Tomorrow she would find a wastebasket. There was nothing more she could do tonight. She might as well go to bed.

She remembered that her nightclothes were in the square suitcase. When she unsnapped the lock and raised the lid, her hands identified the green dress that Dad especially liked. Poor wrinkled dress. She would have to wait until tomorrow when she could see to hang it up.

Janna dug toward the bottom of the suitcase until she found her pajamas. She changed clothes quickly. Once in bed, she closed her eyes tightly while she whispered an urgent prayer for protection. Then she opened them to stare sightlessly at the ceiling. The walls were thin. She could hear the big clock in the parlor striking the hour; she counted. Ten o'clock.

Janna lay in the dark, breathing shallowly as she listened to the sounds of the old house. Suddenly she stiffened. She strained her ears, tense. Something or someone was tapping lightly at the porch window. Was someone planning to break in? The sound was not repeated. After a long interval of silence she heard the scurry of tiny footsteps on the porch roof above her window.

The cane Janna had found next to the front door gave her a small feeling of safety. She had laid it on the bed beside her. At least she had something to defend herself with if she needed to. Her imagination pictured a possible intruder and plotted her defense.

Ever since she could remember, Janna's parents had encouraged her to memorize Scripture verses. She began repeating the first one that came to mind:

"Even though I walk through the valley of the shadow of death, I will fear no evil, for you are with me."

Janna realized that she was repeating the verse

without even thinking about what the words were saying. Her mind was preoccupied with the eeriness of the house.

"I will fear no evil," she forced herself to repeat, "for you are with me. For you are with me. . . For—you—are—with—me—"

Finally Janna slept. Just as she started to dream, her eyes flew open and her mind was instantly alert. Someone was at the window that looked out on the back porch. And it was no tap-tap-tapping this time, but a noisy working with the screen to open or remove it. Janna froze. Her heart pounded and there was a roaring in her ears. She fought panic as she listened.

Slowly she sat up. She couldn't remember the strategy she had planned. Where could she hide? Under the bed? She'd be trapped there. Besides, she couldn't hide and let someone rob her Aunt Agatha's house. She groped beside her for the stick.

She slipped from her bed just as the window was being raised. Just then she heard again the horrifying scream.

4

The Intruder

Janna hid behind the curtains of the other window. From there she could either attack or escape, whichever seemed wiser after she had seen the burglar.

The curtains billowed out and someone, flashlight in hand, threw one leg over the windowsill. The intruder's back was toward Janna. He was about her

size, maybe a little smaller, and looked like he had nothing in his hands but the flashlight. Janna was sure she could handle him, especially if she used her wits. As soon as the prowler was inside the room, she flung aside the curtain and poked the end of her stick into his back.

"Put up your hands!" she said. The intruder stiffened, then slowly raised his arms. The flashlight's beam made a bright circle on the ceiling. Still holding the stick firmly in place Janna reached for the flashlight. "You don't need this," she said. She turned the beam of light on the housebreaker.

"He" was a girl about Janna's age. She wore a baggy yellow and green striped shirt and faded jeans. Her brown hair was pulled back in a ponytail. She wore dingy white sneakers and no socks. On her left wrist was a wide leather band that held a small watch face. Although she seemed to be built a little more solidly than Janna, she was shorter.

While Janna was making her inspection, the girl looked furtively over her shoulder. When she saw that the "gun" was only a cane, she whirled around.

"Hey! What's going on?" she sputtered furiously.

Janna held the stick threateningly in front of her.

"What are you doing, breaking into my aunt's house?"

"So you're the niece!" Her dark eyes flashed. "Your aunt wanted me to stay with you at night. I couldn't get in by the doors 'cause they're all locked. You must be a real scaredy-cat." The girl looked up at Janna with disdain. "You'd better go back to the big city where a policeman sits on every corner."

Janna ignored the remark and relaxed her grip on the stick. "Where's my aunt?"

"In the hospital. She had a stroke day before yesterday. Poor time for you to come visitin'."

Now that Janna was no longer afraid, suspicion returned. "How do I know you're telling the truth? Maybe you're just taking advantage of this time to steal from my aunt." She took a better grip on her stick.

"Do you know your aunt's writin'?"

Janna nodded. Of course she did. Didn't she have a boxful of letters written by Aunt Agatha?

The girl dug into a back pocket.

"Here's the grocery list she gave me," she said, handing over a scrap of paper.

Janna reached to get her glasses from the top of the dresser. When they were in place, she held the flashlight on the list and scanned it.

Salt (two pounds)

Tomatoes (three cans)

Oatmeal (large size)

Dry milk

Oleo

Hand soap

"That looks like Aunt Agatha's writing," she admitted. "But where are the groceries?"

"Outside the kitchen door. If you'll let me, I'll bring them in."

Janna nodded. The girl moved the chair from the door disdainfully.

"How about giving me my flashlight?" The girl held out her hand and Janna returned the flashlight.

She followed the girl as she strode through the

42

hall, into the kitchen, unlocked the door, and stepped outside. In a few seconds she reappeared carrying a grocery sack. She set the sack on a chair. Then she took a candle from a shelf in the kitchen and placed it on the table. After she had lighted the candle, she turned off the flashlight.

Next she started emptying the sack, putting its contents on the table for Janna's inspection: dry milk, oatmeal, three cans of tomatoes, salt, oleo, soap.

"Believe me now?" asked the girl with a flip of her ponytail.

"Where is the hospital where my aunt is? I have to go see her."

"Kind of late, don't you think?"

Janna's face flushed. *Lord, please help me keep from losing my temper,* she prayed. She took a deep breath and slowly let it out.

". . . Besides, she's in intensive care, so you wouldn't be able to see much of her. Maybe you'd just better go home."

"Please, just tell me where the hospital is."

The girl shrugged her shoulders. "In Kay, five miles from here." She began shelving the groceries.

Janna watched as the girl removed each item from the table. Finally Janna spoke, "I didn't find a bathroom anywhere in the house. . . ."

The girl laughed. "That's 'cause there isn't one. There's an outhouse out back. The bathtub is hanging on the wall of the well house. In the winter, Miss Agatha carries it into the kitchen; in the summer she carries it into the well house. Real handy!"

Janna tried to act as if the arrangement were normal, finally asking, "What's your name?"

"Trebla." Its strangeness didn't register with Janna at the moment.

"I'm Janna. . . . What was that screaming just before you came in?"

Trebla looked at Janna in amusement. "Kinda scary, huh? You'll want to be on your guard"—the girl paused dramatically—"for your aunt's cat, Prowler."

"Oh." Janna tried to hide her embarrassment. "Was he hurt?"

"Hurt!" Trebla's amusement turned to disdain. "Can't you even tell when a cat's singin'?"

Janna drew a sharp breath and looked at the stick in her hand.

The girl finished putting up the groceries and lit another candle. "I'm sleeping in the parlor on a cot. I'm supposed to stay until after you have breakfast."

"Don't bother," said Janna. "I can fix my own."

"I told your aunt I would. Besides, you won't be here long, so I won't be out much bother."

Was that a threat? Janna wondered. "How do you know how long I'll be here?"

"With your aunt in the hospital, why would you stay? Besides, the house isn't friendly to strangers." Her eyes narrowed and there was another dramatic pause. "It wants you gone."

It was Janna's turn to show disdain. Falling into an imitation of her friend Brooke, she rolled her eyes upward and said, "I'm sure. Cats may sing, but houses aren't friendly or unfriendly—they're just so much wood and . . . and . . . stone."

"Wanna bet?" Turning to face Janna, Trebla put her hands on her hips. "This house is as old as the hills and so set in its ways that it doesn't take kindly to strangers, especially when they try to change things." With that she picked up one of the candles and walked through the door leading into the hall.

44

Strange girl . . . and come to think of it, strange name, thought Janna. *At least I know one person around here who isn't strange—Aunt Agatha. If only she were here, everything wouldn't seem so odd, or so scary.*

Janna took the remaining candle from the kitchen table and went to her own room.

Trebla hadn't relocked the side door. In spite of Janna's apprehension, her pride kept her from doing it. However, she repositioned the chair against her door. Then she blew out the candle and crawled into bed. She listened to the squeaking of the floor outside her door. Was it someone climbing the steps to the second story or was it merely the groaning of an old house? She shivered as she closed her eyes and forced herself to go to sleep.

The next sound Janna heard was from outside.

"Phoebe, phoebe, phoebe."

She stirred.

The bird in the tree by her window sang more lustily, "Phoebe, phoebe, phoebe."

Janna opened her eyes. The black of night had turned to predawn gray. It was much earlier than she usually got up. Should she roll over and try to go back to sleep? The bird was noisy. Besides, there was much that she wanted to do: explore the house and grounds, go see Aunt Agatha in the hospital, find a swimming pool and a tennis court.

Janna threw back her covers and sat up. She bounced out of bed and searched in her suitcase for her blue shorts outfit.

As she dressed, Janna gazed around the large, sparsely furnished room. Besides the chair she had used to block the door, there were only three other pieces of furniture: the bed, a desk, and a dresser.

45

The bed was an old-fashioned iron one with coil springs topped by a thin cotton mattress. The mirror above the dresser looked cloudy, like the eyes of a very old person. Age had also taken its toll on the wallpaper, once obviously bright with pink roses.

When Janna went into the kitchen she found Trebla already there, eating oatmeal. She hung over her bowl as if guarding it. She roused herself to speak, almost in a friendly tone, "Have some." She waved her spoon at a white enamel pan on the stove behind her. Janna filled her bowl and sat down at the table.

"I didn't cook it on the woodstove," Trebla continued. "It's too much trouble for just a pan of oats. There's a kerosene stove in the well house above the cellar. I'll show you how to use it. Can you get something for lunch? Do you know how to cook?"

"I'll get my own lunch," said Janna, catching herself so that at least her tone was even. She put milk in her oatmeal. She was hungry.

"I'm supposed to show you how to draw water from the well and how to light Miss Agatha's kerosene lamp," Trebla said.

Not only were the people here strange, but their life-styles were, too. Janna felt as though she had stepped back in time. She also noticed Trebla's reference to her aunt by name and felt a twinge of jealousy.

After she had finished her cereal, Trebla rose from the table and got a match. She then motioned Janna—who hesitated momentarily over her oatmeal—to follow her to the parlor where a lamp sat on the mantle of a stone fireplace. Trebla took it down and placed it on a small claw-footed table. The bowl of the lamp was half full of kerosene. A long wick reached from the bottom of the bowl up into the base of the globe.

46

"First, turn this little wheel-shaped handle on the side of the lamp," she said. "That raises the wick so you can light it. Then take off the globe and light the wick" (which Trebla did). "If there's too much wick, it'll blacken the globe, so you might need to turn it down some. To put out the light, turn the wick down even lower and blow into the globe.... Go ahead, blow it out."

Janna started to say she didn't know how, but caught herself when she realized how ridiculous that would sound. She blew hard, perhaps a little too hard, for she saw a trace of a smirk on Trebla's face. But the flame went out.

"If you cup your hand at the top of the globe and blow, it'll go out easier." Then picking up the lamp, she said, "It'll be in the kitchen so we can both use it.... When you're through eating, come out into the well house and I'll show you about the stove and the well and where the key to the cellar's kept. I'm taking the milk to the cellar now. Miss Agatha doesn't have an icebox, so anything that needs to be kept cold is there."

Janna took the last bites of oatmeal from her bowl and followed Trebla out of the kitchen and into the side yard. As Janna stepped into the sunshine, a large gray cat uncurled itself from its warm spot in the sun. It stretched sensuously, then, purring, came to rub against her legs. She bent down and stroked its fur.

"You, big kitty, must be the screamer. Or singer, as Trebla describes your noises."

The cat purred loudly.

"You should be more considerate of city people, though," she told him.

Prowler followed her as she entered the well house.

She glanced around the small room. In the corner to her left was a well with a hand pump. Against the back wall stood a two-burner kerosene stove and an oilcloth-covered table. Above the table a small window with a missing pane looked out into a tree; Janna wondered vaguely if the pane hadn't been knocked out by the branch that passed by the window. The right side of the room featured a door with a hole in the bottom of it, as if someone in anger had once put a foot through it. The door appeared to be firmly shut. (An open padlock hung from a staple on the door facing and a hasp was turned back on the door frame.)

Where was Trebla? She was going to show Janna how to light the stove. Had she gone outside? Janna walked to the door and looked back toward the house. The flowers that gave the dwelling its name had multiplied with the years: Vines carrying small pink roses climbed the fence. A weathered trellis near the kitchen door was covered with them. Having nothing better to cling to, some of them were scaling a corner of the house. Later Janna examined the plant more closely, noting the tiny tendrils going into the cracks in the wood.

Just as Janna raised her eyes to a second story window, she saw the curtain move. Had a hand dropped it into place? It gave her little prickles on the back of her neck to think that she was being watched. Perhaps Trebla had gone upstairs and was watching her furtively.

"Are you going to learn to work the stove or not?"

Janna whirled around. The door with the hole was open. Her hand on the knob, Trebla stood at the top of a flight of stairs that descended, no doubt, into the cellar.

5

Footprints in the Dust

It didn't take Janna long to learn to light the kerosene stove—its fumes were unlike anything she had ever smelled before—and to pump water from the well. And she noted carefully the placement of the key to the cellar, under the stove.

"I'm going to get my camera and look around," she told Trebla.

"Better not go into the barn loft. The ladder's rickety and the loft floor has holes," said Trebla.

Janna returned to the house and Trebla followed as far as the kitchen. In her room, Janna contemplated her suitcases, *Mother would shake her head at this mess if she were here.* She picked up her camera and began to walk out of the room. Pausing at the door, she looked back at her suitcases.

"I guess if I don't hang them up, no one else will," she said out loud. She set the camera down and began to put her clothes away. "Mother would be so proud of you," she told herself.

She put the green dress on a hanger and hung it in the closet. As she did so, she heard footsteps. They seemed to come from the floor above. She stood still.

Creak, creak.

Goose bumps roughed the skin on her arms. She shook herself. Perhaps it was only Trebla on an errand upstairs. She slipped to the kitchen. Trebla had just finished sweeping and was putting the broom in the corner.

"It sounds like someone's upstairs."

"You're imagining things," Trebla answered as she hung up the dustpan. "There's no one there."

The steps began again.

"Hear it?" asked Janna.

"Oh—that's nothing to get excited about. It's the wind, probably, or squirrels in the attic. Or mice. Are you afraid of mice?" Trebla's voice was mocking.

"It didn't sound like squirrels or mice to me and there's not that much wind," Janna objected.

"Suit yourself. An old house is full of noises. Some people even say that Miss Agatha's dead husband haunts this one. Maybe his ghost is walking."

Janna looked at Trebla for a moment to see how serious she was. But Trebla's face didn't give any indication that she was teasing.

Janna thought about pressing the issue, but decided Trebla wouldn't be of much help. She went back to her room, picked up her camera, and left the house. She wanted to get away from the noises and the feeling that someone besides Trebla was in the house.

Almost as soon as Janna got outside, Prowler came up and rubbed against her leg. She sat on the step to stroke his sleek fur, and he purred, arching his back with pleasure. She watched as a yellow striped bee buzzed past her to bury himself in a pink rose.

Finally Janna stood up. "Coming with me?" she asked the cat. Together they sauntered toward the gate behind the house. The path obviously wasn't heavily traveled, for tufts of grass overlapped the stones, and an occasional yellow dandelion shone like a spot of sunshine. At the gate she turned to take a picture of the house. The shadow of one of the dead sycamore trees stretched long, dark arms across the yard.

The house looks as if it knows a hundred secrets, she thought as she took a picture of it. Even the covered windows seemed to be hiding something— or someone.

As Janna and Prowler stepped through the gate into the barn lot, Janna caught a glimpse of a man disappearing around the corner of the barn. She had thought she and Trebla were the only ones at Aunt Agatha's. The man reappeared. This time he carried a metal bucket that jingled as he walked. He was dressed in blue overalls, which hung loosely on his thin frame. A straw hat, ragged with long wear, covered his head.

The man would have passed without speaking if Janna had not called out to him. "Good morning."

"Mornin'," he responded—grudgingly it seemed to Janna. "I reckon you're Miss Agatha's niece. This is a mighty poor time to come visitin'." His speech was jerky and he avoided looking into Janna's eyes. Had he and Trebla agreed to make her unwelcome?

"I didn't know Aunt Agatha had anyone working for her."

"Trebla sees to the house and I take care of things outside."

"I see. My name's Janna Edmundson."

"Mine's Andy Hoskins. . . . Well, I'd best git on about my business," and he hurried off with short, quick steps. As he retreated, Janna noticed that the small white dog that followed close at his heels seemed to hop rather than to trot. She looked more intently. Why, he had only three legs!

Janna turned back to close the wooden gate. As

51

she did so, to her delight, a gray horse came whinnying across the lot toward her. She approached the mare with her hand outstretched. The horse bent its head to nuzzle Janna's palm.

"I'm sorry, Big Boy—or is it ... uh, huh. Sorry, Big Girl. I didn't know you'd expect something. I'll try to bring you some sugar next time." Janna stroked the horse's long, silky nose and then patted its flank.

As Janna ambled on, the horse plodded beside her. The open front of the barn beckoned Janna. She walked from the sunshine into the shadowed building. As her eyes adjusted, she could see that toward the back were rooms enclosed by rough, unfinished lumber. Curious, she lifted a latch to a room on the right. It was empty. Closing it, she turned to a room on the left side. As her eyes adjusted to its darkness, she could make out three bales of hay, half a sack of corn, two battered buckets, a tub of ground feed, and a sack of chicken feed.

Janna eyed the loft and then looked at the cross boards that had been nailed to two of the beams to make a ladder. A room was below this portion of the loft. Janna walked over to its door, which was ajar. A rusty metal hasp jutted out from the door post. Janna gingerly swung it back on itself and the doorpost. She poked her head in the door. Here and there were piles of hay and gunnysacks and ears of dried corn. It was the corn bin, but it looked like it hadn't seen use for some time.

Janna walked back outside. She decided to follow a path that branched from the main one that went into the barn. It led to a shed on the side of the barn. Evidently this was the horse's quarters; it had a water trough and a feed box. The horse followed her to the feed box and nosed around the edges.

Next to the horse's quarters was a room for Aunt Agatha's hens. A white leghorn balanced on a perch just outside its door. It jumped down with a startled squawk and dashed to a clump of buckberry bushes. Janna opened the door and peeked inside. Three open boxes on the wall held nests, and one of them held a hen. Its limp red comb flopped to cover one black, beady eye. The hen stared unblinkingly at her visitor. Janna softly closed the door.

She wanted to go into the loft, but Trebla's warning rang in her ears. She followed the path back into the barn. Prowler continued to trail her. As her eyes adjusted, she walked over to the ladder to the loft and examined it. The cross pieces looked safe.

Suddenly she was surprised by Prowler: He was climbing the ladder. When he reached the top of the ladder he scrambled out of sight. For a moment Janna contemplated the journey of the cat. When he returned to the edge of the loft and looked down as if to see what was keeping her, she decided to follow.

The gray boards were slick and smooth under her hands, worn by many feet. Finally she could see into the loft. Two bales of hay lay diagonally before her.

Cautiously she pulled herself onto the loft floor. She stood and looked around. Here and there was a broken bale of hay. At one end of the loft were stacked the whole bales. The two bales in front of her seemed curiously isolated. Cobwebs festooned the rafters. An alarmed barn swallow startled her when it zoomed out of the loft; then all was quiet. The floor looked solid. Janna wondered why Trebla had warned her about it. Did she think she was unable to climb a ladder just because she came from the city? Or did she, for some reason, hope to keep her out of the loft?

Here and there a shaft of sunlight caught the dust

in the air and lit a spot on the loft floor. They came from holes in an outside wall of the barn. Idly following a shaft of light, Janna peeked through to the outside. She could see the back of the house, the well house, and beyond, to the road.

Janna climbed down the ladder. The cat scrambled after her. Together they walked back out into the sunlight and then to the shed attached to the right side of the barn. There sat a two-wheeled, one-horse vehicle. The ends of the long shafts rested on the ground. The black top was up. Prowler leaped up into the floor of the buggy, then into the seat.

"Mrraow," he said to Janna, inviting her to follow.

"Prowler, I *like* this!" She climbed in and sat down on the soft leather seat. She looked around with pleasure. Then she drew the buggy whip from the holder and pretended to crack it over the back of an imaginary steed. Did Aunt Agatha still use this to drive to town? The buggy was old but seemed to be in good shape. Perhaps her very own mother had ridden in it years ago. Janna could picture her aunt sitting in the driver's seat, reins in hand, as she clucked to the horse to start. And she could see her mother, a small, pigtailed girl, perched beside the woman.

What is Aunt Agatha really like? Janna wondered. *Poor Aunt Agatha. Widowed. Childless. All alone in the world except for me. . . . Why was her husband's ghost said to haunt the house?*

Suddenly Prowler stiffened and jumped from the buggy. Startled, Janna watched as he dashed to a dark corner of the shed. She saw a small, long-tailed mouse streak along the floor and disappear into a hole. Prowler had lost his prey.

Trebla had said that Janna was to get her own lunch, so she decided to see if the hens had laid yet.

54

She climbed out of the buggy and brushed off the seat of her shorts. On her way to the henhouse she stopped to pet the horse. Perhaps she could hitch him to the buggy and that would supply her transportation.

As she came out of the henhouse, two warm white eggs in her hands, she saw a man at the far edge of the horse pen.

"Mr. Hoskins," she called to him. "Does Aunt Agatha still drive the buggy?"

The man didn't answer, nor did he turn to face her.

Perhaps he doesn't hear well, Janna thought. She raised her voice.

"Mr. Hoskins, does Aunt Agatha still use the buggy?" The man quickened his pace until, as he reached the edge of the barn lot, he broke into a run. Janna watched, puzzled. Why would Mr. Hoskins run from her?

Still staring at the spot in the woods where the man had disappeared, Janna went to the edge of the barn lot. There, clearly imprinted in the loose dirt, was the shape of a sharp-toed, smooth-soled boot.

As Janna left the sunlight and opened the back door of the house, gloom settled over her. She slipped down the hall, feeling that she wanted to be as quiet as possible. It seemed that the house was listening.

There is no need to eat here, she thought. Especially since she would cook her eggs on the stove in the well house.

As she crossed from the kitchen to the well house she looked for Prowler. Evidently he had stayed at the barn. Perhaps he was keeping vigil at the mouse hole.

She opened the door to the well house. She hadn't

seen the cellar yet. She descended the narrow stone steps, placing her flattened palms on the wall for balance. The moist coolness of the cellar rose to meet her and her eyes strained to see into the dim light.

Shelves reached from the floor to the ceiling of the cellar and they were filled with jars. Some were empty and coated with the dust of many years. Others were filled with food canned long ago; it was impossible to identify their contents, either by shape or by color.

A few filled jars looked bright and fresh. Aunt Agatha must have canned some recently. Janna's eyes had adjusted to the dimness and now she could see quite well. She examined one jar. It looked like blackberries.

In one corner of the cellar was an old egg crate; cardboard dividers were still stacked in it. Perhaps Aunt Agatha used to sell eggs. Next to the shelves on the floor sat a large wooden box. Janna raised its lid. Old newspapers lined the bottom. At first Janna thought it hadn't been built very well because of the spaces between the boards. But after studying it and recognizing onion skins on the newspaper, she decided that perhaps the box had been designed to allow air to get to its contents, rather than keep it out.

A frog hopped from one damp corner of the dirt floor to another. Suddenly the chilly gloom made Janna want to get back into the sunshine. She hurried up the steps, closed the cellar door, and scrambled her two eggs.

She had just scraped the last bite of egg from her plate when she heard someone knocking on the front door of the house.

She started to call out and then checked herself. She decided to go meet whoever it was and started toward the front of the house. But coming around the corner of the house to meet her was a tall figure whose face broke into a smile when he saw her. It was Mike Morris, The Smile. She felt as if the sun had come out from behind the clouds!

"Hey," he greeted Janna.

" 'Hey'? In Cincinnati we usually say hi," Janna said with a smile.

Mike looked around and behind him. "Doesn't look like Cinncinati to me." He crossed his arms as his face lit up with that smile. "But I suppose I could learn to say hi."

Feeling slightly embarrassed at the smile being directed at her and his quick willingness to accommodate her, Janna shrugged her shoulders. "I guess that's not fair, considering I'm the stranger."

"Well, then, maybe I can teach *you* how to talk country," he said with an exaggerated drawl. "So then you'll sound down-home and won't stand out so much."

Janna frowned. She hadn't thought about how she was coming across to these people.

"Hey, I'm sorry," Mike said quickly. "I didn't mean to make fun of you."

"Oh, no—it's okay. I was just thinking of how one-sided my thinking has been. Everything seems so different, and I'm disappointed that Aunt Agatha couldn't meet me, and it's scary here, and there's no swimming pool or tennis courts, and . . ." Before Janna knew it she was tearing.

Mike pulled a bandanna from his back pocket. "Here, it's clean. The twins—my little sisters—gave it to me as a gift and try to make sure I carry it." He laughed. "They'll be happy to hear it was used."

Janna laughed too as she quickly removed her glasses and wiped her tears. This wasn't how she

57

wanted to show off her eyes; her parents offer of contacts was sounding more attractive. "The twins sound nice." She was grateful for the change of subject.

"Usually, they are," said Mike.

Janna laughed again.

The two started slowly toward the steps into the kitchen. "I told my mother you were here," Mike said, "and she sent me to see if you would like a lift to Kay to see your aunt. We go to the store there. Last night I didn't think to ask you if you knew that she was in the hospital. . . . Did you?"

"No, I didn't. But that's all right. I'd really appreciate the ride. I was worried about how I was going to get to the hospital. . . . When are you going?"

"Mom'll be by any minute to pick us up."

"I'll hurry and get ready. It won't take me long. Maybe I can pick up some stamps too. I brought stationery but forgot stamps."

"Sure," Mike said.

Janna thought he sounded honestly pleased. She hoped he didn't think she was immature for showing her emotions so easily. He made her feel so comfortable, though. She'd have to write a letter to Brooke and tell her about him.

Janna went into the house through the kitchen and dashed into the hall. As she did so, she saw the door to the parlor swing shut. Was there enough wind current for that? Trebla was supposed to be gone. Janna didn't have time to check it out. She didn't want to keep Mrs. Morris waiting.

She flew to her room, grabbed the green dress from the closet, and changed into it. She brushed her short blond hair with a few quick strokes, then snatched up the box containing the white shawl her mother had made for Aunt Agatha. It was gossamer light, lacy and dainty—exactly the sort of thing her mom would make.

As Janna rejoined Mike, he was putting a shiny red bike with straight handle bars and knobby tires into place on top of a red station wagon. Janna and Mike climbed into the back seat. He introduced Janna to his mother and his younger twin sisters, Debra and Deidra, who were sitting in the front seat.

Where are the other redheads? Janna wondered. Like their mother, the twins had light brown hair and no freckles. *Mike must favor his dad.*

"Pshew!" exclaimed Mike.

Janna sniffed. The air in the car was suffocatingly sweet.

"We got perfume for our birthday," Debra announced. "Can you smell it?" she asked, turning around and looking at Janna.

"Mike don't like it," added Deidra, also twisting around to look at their new passenger.

"Mike *doesn't* like it," said Mike gently. "And I just said, 'Who fell in the perfume pond?'" He pulled lightly at Deidra's ponytail.

The girls giggled. "Well, it smells better than goats!" said Debra triumphantly.

Mike looked at Janna and shook his head. "Oooh, below the belt." And he doubled over in his seat.

"Bubba, you're silly," said Deidra.

Janna could see the near hero worship in the two faces that turned toward Mike. She thought of Claude and Kerri and Lisa. She missed them. But Aunt Agatha needed her.

Mrs. Morris caught Janna's eye in the mirror. "Don't mind them," she said with a quick smile. (Again Janna saw no resemblance to Mike.)

59

"Have you known Aunt Agatha long?" asked Janna.

"All my life," answered Mrs. Morris. "Both my husband and I grew up here. We left to go to college. He taught for a while in Springfield, but we decided that we wanted to move back to the country, so here we are. I guess Miss Agatha's always lived here."

"Has she always lived in the same house?"

"As far as I know," said Mrs. Morris. "I think her grandfather made claim to the land back in the 1800s."

"I wonder what relation he would be to me?" Janna said out loud.

"Let me think. . . . Your great-great-grandfather."

"Wow," Janna said. "I never thought about my great-great-grandfather before."

"Your aunt took care of her parents in their old age; they were your great-grandparents. She didn't marry while they were alive. She married a couple years after her mother died. But her husband died not many years after that. He was a handsome man."

"Did you know his ghost haunts the house?" asked Debra excitedly.

"He played the violin. And sometimes violin music is heard coming from the house," added Deidra, her eyes wide.

"And he hid a fortune somewhere in the house!" said Debra.

"Oooooooo, ghost stories and hidden treasure legends—they know 'em all," said Mike, looking at the twins and moving his hands as if they were ghosts floating in the air.

"If the house is haunted, it's by Miss Agatha's memories," said Mrs. Morris. "Several generations of your family have lived there, Janna. Poor Miss

Agatha has had a lonely life, I'm afraid. I know she's been looking forward to your coming."

"Do you know the girl my aunt asked to stay nights with me? Her name is Trebla—I don't know her last name."

"Trebla Wooten," said Mike. "She lives about a mile and a half down the road from your aunt's place. She helps Miss Agatha around the house."

"Trebla," repeated Janna. She started to say it was a strange name, but decided to ask if it was a common name in Missouri.

Mike laughed. "We may be different, but not that different." When he saw Janna's embarrassment, he touched her hand and winked.

"They're a strange family," said Mrs. Morris. "Her father named her Trebla. It's Albert spelled backwards. He wanted a boy and decided to call him Albert. When his wife had a girl, he couldn't give up wanting a boy, so he gave her the boy's name spelled backwards."

"Nothing like feeling welcome, huh?" said Mike, making a face.

Janna was silent, thinking.

"There are just the two of them," added Mrs. Morris. "Trebla and her father."

"He drinks a lot," said Mike quietly.

"They're real poor," volunteered Debra.

"You should see the house they live in," Deidra added. "It's just a shack: broken windows covered with boards—"

"Deidra, shush," said Mrs. Morris.

The twin turned to face the front, her head bowed.

"Lester Wooten (they call him 'Woot') came from a good family," Mrs. Morris continued. "Trebla was about six months old when her mother left and never came back. Mr. Wooten drank before that, but when his wife left he seemed to go to pieces."

It occurred to Janna that she was the same age when her parents were killed as Trebla was when her mother left.

Mrs. Morris slowed the car and parked before a two-story gray stone building, the Kay Municipal Hospital.

"We have several errands to run and we'll be back in about an hour and a half," she said.

"Thanks so much for thinking of bringing me," Janna said to Mrs. Morris. "I've been waiting all my life to meet my aunt."

"Actually, it was Mike's idea," Mrs. Morris said, looking at her son with an expression of amusement.

Janna looked at Mike. "Aw, Mom. I wasn't ready for that—below the belt!" And he doubled over, but not before Janna noticed the redness creeping up his neck. She looked at the twins, who were watching the routine, and whispered, "You were right: Silly." But as she opened the car door and stepped out, she was pleased.

As the Morrises pulled away from the curb, Janna walked toward the entrance of the hospital. Her heart quickened with anticipation. She could hardly believe that the meeting she had dreamed about was finally going to take place. Her dearest wish was about to be fulfilled. Would Aunt Agatha be glad to see her? Did the meeting mean as much to her as it did to Janna? Janna could hardly wait to find out.

6

A Visit to Kay

The hospital was small and Janna had no trouble locating the information desk. A crisply uniformed nurse directed her down the hall. Her excitement continued to build as she walked. The tap, tap of her hurrying footsteps rang loudly against the subdued atmosphere of the corridor. The hospital hush contrasted sharply with the mounting emotion inside her. In sudden self-consciousness she began to tiptoe. Her cheeks were flushed and she tingled with anticipation.

She pushed through a heavy swinging door. On the other side of the door sat a nurse who evidently was in charge of the intensive care ward. Janna again identified herself.

"In this ward we must limit visits to five minutes, and no more than one visit an hour," said the nurse.

"I'll watch the time," promised Janna. Then slowly and quietly she walked down the shiny tiled hall. Some of the doors she passed were closed; others stood ajar. The murmur of voices issued from some of the rooms.

Worrying thoughts raced through her mind. Would Aunt Agatha know who she was? She knew nothing of the aftereffects of a stroke. Would the woman be able to hear? Would Janna be able to talk to her?

She saw that the door to Aunt Agatha's room stood open. She paused at the entrance and looked in. The room was bare of flowers. No stack of get-well cards crowded the bedside table. In the hospital bed she saw a woman, white-gowned and still. A heart monitor was attached to her chest.

Then she noticed how thin the woman was, how pale the wrinkled face was. Her hair was sparse and gray—not blonde, like her picture. Pulled back in a small bun, its severity made the face seem all angles. Like Briar Rose Manor, her aunt had changed over the years.

But this was her own flesh and blood! And she seemed so frail . . . so alone. Janna's head grew giddy with happiness. Her heart swelled, filled with an aching affection for her aunt. She longed to embrace the motionless form and stir it to a response to her joy.

Sudden compassion for the old woman flooded over Janna. Janna must take care of her. She *would* take care of her. *Never again will Aunt Agatha be alone,* she vowed.

The girl stepped shyly into the room and the woman's brown eyes flickered open. Aunt Agatha turned toward her.

"Aunt Agatha, I'm Janna."

The brown eyes of the shrunken old woman came to life. "Come in, child! We've waited long enough for this meeting!" Aunt Agatha's left arm lay useless at her side, but she beckoned with her right.

Janna flew to her aunt, arms outstretched. She leaned down and awkwardly hugged the figure on the bed. Aunt Agatha was long and thin and her shoulder blades were like bony wings.

She's tall, too—like me, Janna thought.

"I'm so sorry I couldn't give you a better welcome than this, but then 'The best laid schemes o' mice an' men / Gang aft a-gley.'"

When the old woman noticed the puzzled look on Janna's face, she waved her good hand. "Sorry, honey—You've probably heard it 'The best laid plans of mice and men / often go astray.' . . . Which mine did."

"Just finally being with you is enough," Janna said.

Aunt Agatha was silent for a few seconds, scrutinizing the girl. "You look very much like your mother. She was a lovely woman. You have the same sweet smile . . . and behind those glasses, the same eyes—"

Janna self-consciously pushed her glasses up on her nose.

Just then a nurse appeared. "You must go now."

"I'll stay in the waiting room and I'll see you again in an hour," Janna promised her aunt.

Aunt Agatha smiled and nodded. "Thank you for coming, dear."

When Janna sat down in the waiting room she realized that she had left the gift in Aunt Agatha's room without telling her about it. Oh, well, she'd see her again in an hour. As she waited she turned page after page of the magazines she found stacked neatly on a table. But they might as well have been in a foreign language, for she scarcely recognized what her eyes saw.

The second visit passed too quickly, with time only for Janna to present Aunt Agatha with the shawl and her mother's greeting. However, as Janna left the room the nurse told her that the doctor had said that her aunt would be moved from intensive care the next day if she continued to improve.

When she went again to the waiting room, Janna found that Mike was waiting for her.

"How was your aunt?" he asked as they walked down the hall.

For a moment the question didn't register. Janna had longed for the meeting with her aunt for years. Now that it was over, she felt numb.

"Oh . . . she may be taken out of intensive care tomorrow." And then Janna was lost in thought.

As Janna got in the car, a new smell hit her. It wasn't perfume, but she had recently smelled it. It came from the back of the station wagon, full of bulky sacks of groceries, a sack of ground grain, and a salt block. Of course, animal feed. She had smelled it in one of the sheds of her aunt's barn.

"Thank you for bringing me to town, Mrs. Morris," said Janna.

"We were glad to do it."

As they were headed out of town, Janna exclaimed, "Oh, no, I forgot stamps!"

Mike grinned and pulled a small sheet of stamps out of his shirt pocket.

"Oh, you remembered! Thank you."

"It wasn't hard. I check the post office for information on first-day covers."

"Huh?" said Janna.

"I do a little stamp collecting. Sometimes when a new stamp is going to be printed, I buy a first printing of it. A first-day cover is the new stamp on an envelope with some special artwork, usually of the stamp, the date the stamp was issued, and maybe some background on the stamp."

"Oh." Had it been at another time, Janna would

have pursued the subject. As it was, her mind was on her meeting with her aunt.

"Do you like bikes?" asked Mike.

When Janna gave him a quizzical look, he quickly explained: "I have two. If you don't mind the ride, you can use one of them to go see your aunt whenever you want."

"Oh, yes, thank you!"

"But you might want to change first."

She nodded, with a grateful smile; her mind had gone back to her aunt. Janna would have to give up the idea of wearing a dress to visit her aunt; she wondered vaguely what kind of impression that would make on her. However, by the time they got to Briar Rose, she had accepted the thought that her aunt would rather see her than what she was wearing.

At the Morris farm, Mike led Janna to a small tin shed. Leaning against one side of it was a sturdy bicycle with balloon tires and a large carrier on the front.

"This was my old bike that I used to make deliveries with. You may have to walk it up a hill or two, but at least you won't be carrying any weight in the basket. It's my spare now, since I got my ATB and outfitted it with a special basket, one I can get on and off a lot eaiser."

As he pushed the bike toward the front of the house, a tiny brown goat came frolicking and bleating toward him. It playfully butted against his leg.

"He's cute!" exclaimed Janna, reaching down to scratch the head of the kid. Feeling two bumps on its head, she parted the stiff brown hair with her fingers to see them.

"Horns-to-be," said Mike, in answer to her look. He, too, stroked the kid. Their hands touched and

Janna felt as if a thousand sparkles tingled in her veins.

"Kids make good pets," said Mike.

"Aunt Agatha's hired man has a pet that I feel sorry for. He has a three-legged dog."

"Yeah, I know Mutt."

"Do you know what happened to his leg?"

"He got it broken so Andy just cut it off—"

"Ooooh! Sick! He just cut it off? He didn't take it to a vet?"

"I guess that does sound kind of cruel. But some people around here just have to make do. Can't afford a vet for their pets. . . . He gets along all right on the other three, though."

"Still . . . " She shivered, and then picked up her earlier subject. "Mike, do you know whether or not anyone besides Trebla and Mr. Hoskins work for Aunt Agatha?"

"That's all. Every once in awhile your aunt takes a quart of goat milk, and I've never noticed anyone else around the place. There's not much work to be done. . . . Why do you ask?"

"Oh, it's probably the sounds of an old house. And I guess city noise just hides a lot of that."

Mike nodded.

Janna bent slightly toward Mike and sniffed. "I like your cologne."

His usual smile was shy. "Makes up for the goat smell. My customers may like goat milk, but I've gotta think about people like Ned . . . and city folk."

"Come by to see me soon, okay?" Janna said as she straddled the bike. She noticed the seat was just a little high, but she liked the thought of it being adjusted for someone taller than she was.

"I'll be by in the morning when I do my milk route,"

Mike said. He picked up a small rock and threw it down the driveway. "Janna, I—"

Janna turned to him.

"Oh, nothing," he said. "See you tomorrow."

She started peddling toward Briar Rose Manor.

I wonder what he was going to say, Janna thought.

Mike stood in the driveway watching as she left. Feeling his eyes on her, she turned to wave goodbye. But the combination of height on the seat, gravel on the road, and a boy's bike was too much to keep under control while waving and looking back. The bicycle wobbled, angled toward the ditch, and overturned.

As she cried out, she groaned inwardly. *I think I'll die! First I cry in front of him and now this!*

In a few giant strides Mike was by her side. "Are you all right?"

"Oh, Mike, when I left Ohio I could ride a bike," wailed Janna.

Mike's expression of concern turned into a laugh. Janna hadn't meant to be funny, but when Mike laughed, she could see the humor in her remark. "Well, I could!" she said firmly.

As he helped her up he said, "I'm sorry, Janna. I should have told you everything about this bike. It has ground magnets."

"*Ground magnets?*"

"Yep. Now the car, my dad would tell you, used to have wood magnets. But when we had the right front fender fixed after it was attracted to the corner of the house, that took 'em right out."

Now Janna laughed. "You're just trying to make me feel better."

"Would you like to go for ice cream tonight?"

Janna stopped brushing herself off. "What?"

"That's what I was going to ask you back there but I had a nerve failure." He shrugged with a grin. "Around these parts everyone believes that ice cream makes a body feel better. Just ask the twins."

She smiled, and then rubbing her elbow asked, "Do we have to go on bikes?"

She was surprised when he said no. "You drive?" Janna asked. "Why do you ride a bike everywhere if you can drive?"

"Oh, most of my route is bunched together, so I ride a bike to help my wind, my breathing—I run cross-country. Like the coach tells us," said Mike, swelling his chest and pointing his finger, " 'Boys, a car will slow you down!' " He laughed with Janna. "Anyway, I can usually get the car if I really need to." Giving her The Smile, he said, "I'll need to around seven tonight."

She nodded. Feeling herself beginning to blush, she blurted, "I won't get my license until . . . uh, later." Somehow she got on the bike and began to pedal away. She was sure he thought she was an infant. At the same time, she was almost sure he liked her. When she knew she was out of earshot, she shouted, "Mikey likes me!"

7

"Hospitality" at the Manor

Trebla was fixing supper when Janna reached her aunt's: scrambled eggs, canned tomatoes, and a jar of blackberries from the cellar.

As Janna emptied the blackberries into a bowl she spilled some juice on the oilcloth-covered table. She watched as it spread: a rich, red-purple puddle on a white background.

"Clumsy!" exploded Trebla. "Get a rag and mop up the mess!"

"I didn't do it on purpose!" flashed Janna. She felt her face grow hot. She had decided to be friendly to Trebla and had even intended to tell her of the visit with Aunt Agatha. But now her dislike for Trebla rose like gall in her throat. She wouldn't share with her if she were the last person on earth.

Janna grabbed the dishcloth and slapped it down in the middle of the purple liquid. A shower of droplets splashed over the dishes and flatware surrounding the puddle.

Trebla snorted in derision.

The anger that seethed inside Janna exploded. She hurled the juice-filled cloth at Trebla, but Trebla was quick, almost practiced, in ducking the drippy mess. It hit the wall and fell to the floor; drops of juice ran down the wall toward the floor.

71

Janna yelled, "Mop it up yourself!" She wheeled around and stomped out the door, slamming it behind her. She stormed down the path toward the barn. When she reached the shed, she climbed into the buggy. Tears of anger and self-pity burned her eyes.

Trebla has just spoiled what was turning out to be the best day of my life, seethed Janna. She thought again about the juice incident. Of Trebla's derision. Of Trebla ... *a dumb name ... but she hadn't chosen it—"Nothing like feeling welcome," Mike had said.* And if her mother had seen her temper tantrum she would have been disappointed and hurt, especially if she had heard what home was like for Trebla. Janna was glad her mother hadn't seen her. Of course, Jesus had. He was disappointed in her, she was sure.

Tears came again. But this time they were tears of shame. She sat huddled on the leather seat of the buggy. Finally she slipped to her knees.

"Dear Lord," she prayed, "I don't know why Trebla dislikes me so. You know how hard it is for me to hold my temper. Please forgive me for acting like I did. And please help me to keep from saying things I shouldn't say. . . . Please bless Trebla and help her and her dad. Help him to accept her for who she is. And help me do the same. Thank You, Father." Janna rose to her feet. She didn't know how her request would be answered, but she felt better for having prayed.

Janna heard a car drive up and stop in front. She had forgotten about going for ice cream with Mike. As she ran toward the house, she waved at him. She ran into her room and changed her clothes; in the kitchen she splashed water on her face, noticing the

72

faint purple stain on the wall before she headed for the front door.

As they drove to town, Janna found herself telling Mike what had happened at supper. He was such a good listener. He even told her that he sometimes had problems with his temper, too.

When they got back to Briar Rose Manor, Janna thanked him for the ice cream and the good talk. It was just what she needed. And they had agreed that ice cream for Trebla couldn't hurt.

When Janna stepped into the house, all was quiet. She saw that Trebla's door was closed. She placed her peace offering at her door and knocked.

"Trebla, we brought you some ice cream." There was no sound from the room, but Janna didn't knock again.

Janna took a kerosene lamp from the kitchen and went to her room. Even though she had had a long day, she was wide awake. She dug in her suitcase until she found her diary, a pen, and writing paper. For her, writing in her diary was another way of praying. She often stopped to pray about the things she wrote about.

She thought for a moment and then began writing of her first night and day at Briar Rose Manor. She wrote about meeting Aunt Agatha. She stopped to pray for her. She wrote about Mike and how she felt about him. She prayed that God would be part of their relationsip. She wrote of the guilt she felt because of her bad attitude toward Trebla and she prayed about that. She knew that she wasn't acting like a Christian.

By the time she had finished, it was almost dark. She lighted the lamp and set it on the dresser. Then she settled down in the circle of lamplight to write a letter home. She tried to make it entertaining, without relating anything that would worry her mom and dad. She wrote about Aunt Agatha's hospitalization, but that she was improving. She told them of the Morrises and their help. She also added that she wasn't alone in the house. She said nothing of the mysterious happenings at Briar Rose Manor.

As Janna thought of the Edmundsons, she became homesick. She could imagine the friendliness of their brightly lighted house. She needed some of that warmth from people who had loved her all of her life.

Dad is reading the newspaper, Janna thought. *Mom is probably leafing through a magazine. Kerri and Claude might be working on a jigsaw puzzle and playing with Baby Lisa at the same time.*

The scene in her mind was a cheerful contrast to the dark, creaky house where she was. She wondered wistfully if they missed her. How she longed to be with them! She and Aunt Agatha were blood relatives, but the Edmundsons were her love-family. She was filled with loneliness.

After writing her family, Janna wrote a quick note to Brooke. She told her all about Mike, including how she had embarrassed herself in front of him twice in one day. She knew Brooke would understand how she felt.

Finally Janna changed into her pajamas and knelt to say her prayers. She turned back her covers, blew out the lamp, and climbed into bed. The odor of the kerosene smoke hung in the air, and Janna tucked her nose under the covers.

During the night Janna awoke. She listened intently, thinking that maybe a noise woke her up. She heard nothing. Then she realized hunger pangs

gnawed at her stomach. Only ice cream for supper hadn't been enough—another consequence of her temper. But she knew that she couldn't go back to sleep with her stomach hurting. She decided to get some crackers from the kitchen. That would satisfy her until morning.

Janna got out of bed. Through the uncurtained window on the door at the end of the hall the bright moonlight flowed in a white stream.

She had no trouble finding the crackers. Her only mishap occurred when she knocked over a chair as she moved from the cupboard to the door. She stood motionless for a moment, hoping that she hadn't awakened Trebla.

She stepped into the hall to return to her room. Then she froze with a choked scream. A white-sheeted figure was motionless midway up the stairs. Janna shrank back into the kitchen doorway. The apparition glided up the steps with not so much as a creak. It was as if it skimmed above them.

When Janna could no longer see the specter, she ran down the hall to her room. She closed her door swiftly, then leaned, trembling, against it.

"There *are* no ghosts," she told herself through chattering teeth. Of course there are no ghosts. Then what was it she had just seen? She shivered. Only a ghost could climb those squeaky steps soundlessly. Ghost or no ghost, she wanted her door as securely barred as possible. She placed the chair tightly against it. That wouldn't keep a spirit out, but. . . *were* there ghosts? She still had the crackers. Though she no longer felt hungry, she ate several.

Sleep seemed impossible as she lay in bed, tense and listening. Did she hear footsteps above? Were

76

the stairs creaking now? Finally Janna fell into a restless, dream-harried sleep.

The sun hadn't yet risen when Janna awakened. The phoebe in the tree outside her window was singing its repetitious good morning song. She stretched. It was too early even for breakfast, but she didn't think she could go back to sleep.

As she lay reviewing the almost unbelievable scene of the night before, her courage returned. She wanted to get well-acquainted with the house, and this was a good time. It was beginning to get light out so Janna got up and dressed quickly. She moved the chair from her door. She noticed the ice cream was gone from in front of Trebla's door. She walked quietly down the hall and stood at the foot of the stairway. Taking a deep breath, she climbed the steps to the second floor.

The room at the top of the stairs was obviously a storeroom, overflowing with a collection of what her mother might consider just so much rubbish: Stacks of old magazines and newspapers made tall, uneven pillars that leaned against each other for support. Innumerable boxes cluttered the floor. Some were empty, some were full. To Janna it looked both interesting and reassuring: interesting because it might reflect what her aunt liked and reassuring because her aunt did not appear to make neatness a priority.

Then she walked slowly and quietly down the hall toward the front of the house. She opened the door to the library. In the light of day the volumes lining the shelves looked old and faded. Almost without noticing it, she passed the monstrous desk; it was the books that drew her. From floor to ceiling they covered two entire walls. She pulled out one musty book after another, blowing dust from the top of each as she drew it out. She read their dimmed titles curiously, titles she had never heard of. She tucked two volumes under her arm for nighttime perusal. As an afterthought, she glanced in the closet; it held some nondescript clothing. Finally she left the room.

She looked briefly into the room across the hall from the library: There was Myrtle, the sheet-covered dress-form that had given her such a fright when she searched for Aunt Agatha that first night. Several pieces of furniture were draped with sheets, filling the room with bulky white humps. Before, she had been too occupied with the figure of the dress-form even to notice them. It was a good thing: Even now they gave a spooky appearance to the room.

Janna tried the door to the last room, across the hall from the top of the stairs. It wouldn't give. She turned the knob the opposite direction and pushed again—the door was locked!

As if repelled by the locked door, Janna bolted for the stairs. Hastening down the steps, she again had the almost overpowering impulse to whirl and look behind her; again she felt that her every move was being watched. The stillness made her skin prickle.

Suddenly eager for company, Janna hurried down the stairs and into the kitchen. No Trebla. Janna headed for the well house when she noticed a note on the table: "Got chores at home. Here's breakfast." The note was under a bowl. A box of cereal, milk, and a peach were beside the bowl.

Janna made brief work of her breakfast, for without company she was eager to escape the confines of being inside. She would go for a bike ride; she needed the practice, she thought. As she was peddling out of the driveway, she saw Mike riding toward her.

She could see quart bottles of goat's milk in his basket.

"Hey—I mean, hi," he called.

Janna rode to meet him, smiling. "Hey. Can I tag along?"

"Sure."

Janna rode with Mike until he had made his last delivery. When the basket was empty they returned to Briar Rose Manor.

"That was fun," Janna said. "Could we do it again tommorow?"

"Sure thing. I'll come by about the same time." He toyed with the gears on his handlebars. "Last night was fun too. . . . Did I already say that?"

She laughed. "Twice. But I like hearing it."

"Well, I gotta go now," Mike said. "See you later."

"Bye." She smiled.

He turned his bike around and sped for home.

As Janna parked the bike, she saw Andy Hoskins, the hired man. He was nailing a loose board on the henhouse. The sharp hammer blows rang in the air. Janna remembered when he fled into the woods yesterday. Or had it been him? She was determined to find out. She strolled toward the henhouse. Prowler, tail held high, joined her.

"Mr. Hoskins," Janna called.

The man stopped pounding and turned to face Janna.

"I wonder why you ran from me yesterday when I called to you. Had I offended you?"

The man looked at her, obviously puzzled.

"Don't know what you're talkin' about."

"Just before lunch you were in the horse pen. I called to ask if Aunt Agatha still used her buggy. You didn't answer, but ran away into the woods."

79

"It weren't me, Miss." His voice was emphatic but his eyes refused to meet Janna's. "Don't know who it coulda been, but 'tweren't me."

"I was sure that it was. . . . But I guess I was mistaken."

"There's strange doin's around here. I've heard there are ghosts. Might be there are." He shrugged. "Anyway, 'tweren't me."

For lunch Janna took an apple from a box she had found under the cupboard and decided to buy a hamburger in town instead of preparing one at the house. As she rode to Kay she puzzled over the hired man's denial. Had he lied to her? She decided she would do some detective work. *I'll look to see whether or not he wears cowboy boots.*

It didn't take long to get to Kay. Since the noon rush was over at the Snak Shack, Janna's order was filled quickly. She liked her hamburger: It was so thick with lettuce, tomato, onion, and pickle that she could hardly stretch her mouth over it. She was contentedly full when she parked the bicycle and entered the hospital.

"I'm here to see my aunt, Mrs. Mitchell," she told the nurse at the desk. "Has she been moved from intensive care yet?"

The receptionist checked a list on her desk. "Mrs. Mitchell has been moved to room 202. You may see her anytime."

Janna hurried to the stairs. She sprinted up the steps and turned to the right when she reached the top.

Visiting hours were in full swing. People hurried past her. One woman carried a bouquet of daisies. Janna decided that the next time she came that she would bring flowers to Aunt Agatha, a bunch of pink roses to remind her of home.

The clock at the nurse's station read 2:04. Today she would have a good visit with Aunt Agatha. Yesterday they had had so little time together that it was far from satisfying. But today would be different.

She stepped inside the open door of room 202 and stood for a few seconds without speaking. The frail old woman again seemed to be asleep. Her face was as colorless as the white sheet that covered her. The gossamer shawl, the gift of Janna's mother, was wrapped around her shoulders. Janna studied her aunt: It was hard to see any resemblance between her and the photograph Janna had looked at so many times that her memory could reproduce it vividly.

"Aunt Agatha," Janna said softly, taking a few steps into the room. The woman's eyes opened instantly and Janna realized that she hadn't been asleep.

"I'm so glad you've come," she said. "Now we can get acquainted. We had too little time yesterday."

Janna bent to kiss her aunt's withered cheek, then she pulled a chair close to the bed. She covered the woman's gnarled right hand with her own. The hand was cool to her touch.

"Please tell me everything you know about my parents," she begged.

"First I'd like you to crank up my bed a little, if you would," said Aunt Agatha. Janna did so, then again took her seat.

"I knew your mother since her birth," said Aunt Agatha. "She was the only child of my only brother. He was fifteen years younger than I, so he seemed more like a son than a brother. Your father's parents—fine people they were—moved to Mineville

81

when he was in high school (so I didn't know him before that). It's too bad his parents didn't live long enough for you to know them. We're the only two left, as far as I know. That makes you very special to me." Aunt Agatha's warm brown eyes shone with affection.

Janna sat entranced as Aunt Agatha told story after story about her parents and grandparents. She spoke hardly a word other than an occasional question or exclamation. How she wished that she had brought paper and a pen with her so she could take notes! The next time she would.

When a nurse entered with a tray holding three small white paper cups of medicine, Janna glanced at her watch. It seemed incredible that she had been with Aunt Agatha for over an hour. The woman's voice had slowed and Janna realized that the visit had tired her. Janna felt a twinge of guilt. She arose and replaced the chair against the wall.

"Thank you so much, Aunt Agatha. I had better go now, but I'll come again tomorrow." She bent and kissed her aunt's forehead. As she left the room, she turned for a last good-bye. Her aunt waved and smiled around the thermometer the nurse had put in her mouth.

Later Janna couldn't even remember peddling home. When she got there she was still so exhilerated that she didn't want to spoil her mood by going into the the stern, old gray house. She wasn't sure she wanted to meet Trebla, either. She stole through the back door and went straight to her room where she got her diary and pen. Then she slipped out again. She knew exactly the place where she would review her visit with Aunt Agatha. She wanted to record all the information she had received before she forgot any of it.

She hurried to the shed beside the barn and climbed into the old buggy. She seemed to be the only person on the premises. As she opened her diary to the first blank page, Prowler jumped into the buggy and onto the seat beside her. He lay down, purring.

For the next hour time stood still. Janna wrote almost steadily, pausing only long enough to remember something more that Aunt Agatha had told her. Finally, after hungering for it for so long, she was beginning to feel that she was part of a family.

Janna was gazing absently at the open shed door when a man in a green cape crept by. His stealthy movements suggested to her that he was where he had no right to be. She had no desire to confront him, so ominous he seemed. She stepped down from the buggy and hurried to the door to see if he was still in sight. She stood concealed in the shadows as she watched him scurry across the lot and melt, green cloak and all, into the trees.

After he had disappeared, she followed his path across the barn lot, but she found no tracks. Questions filled her mind. Had he worn high-heeled boots? Was he the same man she had seen before? Did he represent a menace to Aunt Agatha? Why did each of the mysterious trespassers take the same route to vanish in the dark woods?

Prowler, unconcerned with mysteries and intrigues, purred and rubbed against her ankles.

Janna returned to the buggy to get her diary, then started toward the house. As she swung open the squeaky gate, she stopped suddenly; she felt the hair stiffen on the back of her neck. Violin music! It was coming from the house!

8

Prowler's Surprise

Reluctantly Janna entered the house. Sudden silence met her. The strains of violin music had died in the air. She stood in the hall, listening.

Bong. Bong. Bong. . . . The old clock in the parlor struck six times; then the only sound was its ticking. Janna went into the empty kitchen where she prepared a quick supper of a peanut butter and honey sandwich and a glass of milk. After she had eaten she stepped from the kitchen to go to the well house. As she did so, the big gray cat came down the path toward her.

"Here, Prowler," she called. "Kitty, Kitty, Kitty." When the cat approached, she saw that he carried something in his mouth. Something small and brown. Something that squeaked.

Janna hurried to the cat and knelt beside him.

"What do you have, Prowler?"

He placed his treasure before her as if it were a gift.

"It's a baby rabbit!" Tenderly Janna picked up the tiny terrified creature. Its round dark eyes stared imploringly at her. It lay unresisting as she examined it for injuries. No blood. No wounds. Perhaps it was only frightened. She would care for it, and it would be her pet.

She felt that she owed Prowler something for the rabbit, so she poured milk into a saucer and set it on the floor of the well house.

"I'll fix a nest for you," she told the rabbit. "I'll find a box and I'll make it soft with grass. I wonder what I should feed you. Milk?"

She remembered some empty shoe boxes among the stacks of magazines and clutter in the room upstairs. She was sure that Aunt Agatha would let her use one. Holding the little brown rabbit in one hand cupped against her chest, she entered the house.

As she started up the stairs she remembered the ghostly figure she had seen the night before. It had not made a sound. No thud of footsteps, no squeaking of stairs. Janna shivered. But she wanted a box for Bunny. *Besides, there are* no *ghosts,* she told herself.

On the other hand, how could a flesh-and-blood person glide noiselessly up these old steps?

She wondered. . . . Experimentally she walked on the edges of the steps, next to the wall, instead of on the worn centers. This was much quieter, she decided with satisfaction. So a living, physical body could ascend quietly.

In the room at the top of the stairs she soon found an empty shoe box. Just right, she decided. Before it got dark she must line the box with grass. Outside she found a spot deep in clover. She dropped to her knees and set the box beside her. Pulling with vigor for her new pet, she soon had the box half full. The small rabbit burrowed into its green nest.

Now for food. She was warming milk for the rabbit when Trebla appeared at the well house door. Janna noticed she still wore the baggy green and yellow striped top she had been wearing Monday night when she came through Janna's window.

"Oh, hi. I'm heating milk for a baby rabbit Prowler brought in. Do you know where there's an eyedropper I can use to feed it?"

Trebla nodded. When she returned with an eyedropper, Janna asked if she would like to see the rabbit. She shook her head, but her face was expressionless. "No. It won't live caught. Wild things never do."

Janna bolted to her room. With an air of determination she squirted warm milk into the rabbit's mouth. "You will live, you will live." The rabbit drooled until the fur around its mouth was plastered. Finally Janna was sure it had got enough. She wiped the dribbles off its mouth with a tissue. Then she sat on the edge of her bed with the soft, warm little body cupped in her hand. With one finger she stroked its tiny form. Its brown fur felt like satin. Janna's eyes were tender as she held its softness against her cheek. Finally she placed it in its clover nest and set the box on the floor near the closet.

After Janna had settled the bunny, she reread the letter she had found in the mailbox that afternoon. It was from her mother; she had written it the night Janna had left. Of course, it didn't have any news, but her mother was telling Janna she already missed her. Janna stared out her window and noticed it was twilight—the loneliest time of day in the country. It should have made her feel good that she had received a note from home so soon.

Home? She would never go home again except to visit. This big gray house was her home now. A tear trickled slowly down her cheek. Lisa would grow up and she wouldn't be there to watch; the baby would finally forget her.

Janna wrote in her diary, emptying her grief on the receptive white page. And she prayed, sure that Jesus understood and sympathized. Finally she felt better. By the time she was ready to write to the Edmundsons, she was able to hide her unhappiness and again made no mention of anything that might worry her parents. She told of her visit to Aunt Agatha. She told of Mike's generosity in lending his bicycle, and described him, how he was tall and redheaded and ran track. For Claude and Lisa and Kerri she drew a funny sketch of Prowler and his gift of the bunny. When she reread the letter she was glad she had not burdened her beloved family with her loneliness.

Turning her chair so that the lamplight shone over her shoulder, Janna opened the first of the two books that she had carried downstairs. As she skimmed

87

them, she found them boring. One was the life of Ulysses S. Grant, the other a history of beekeeping. She yawned as she flipped the pages. She might as well go to bed.

She barricaded her door and took a last peek at the tiny rabbit buried in the clover bed. She blew out the kerosene lamp and wrinkled her nose at the now familiar fumes.

Hours later Janna awakened, suddenly alert. She lay still and listened. At first she heard nothing; then she caught the distinct sound of footsteps on the bare floor above. Should she investigate? The chill of fear swept through her. She pulled the sheet close up under her chin as if hiding under it gave her safety.

I'm not about to go snooping at night, she decided.

Then she sat up. *Did I push the chair against the door?* She couldn't remember. She crawled out of bed and groped her way to the door. The chair was firmly wedged against it. She returned to her bed and finally slept.

"Phoebe, phoebe, phoebe."

Janna opened her eyes and yawned. The sun's first rays were just beginning to brighten the trees on the hilltop across the valley. Mother would be amazed to hear how early her rising hour had become. She'd have to tell the family about her feathered alarm clock who thought that her name was Phoebe instead of Janna.

Might as well get up, she urged herself.

She didn't like to prowl upstairs at night, but early morning seemed safe enough. Besides, in the early morning she wasn't likely to run into Trebla.

She pulled on a pair of jams and a baggy T-shirt she had appropriated from her dad.

In daylight, the upstairs looked ordinary enough,

88

not mysterious at all. The storeroom was just as full as before. It must have taken years to accumulate the clutter it contained. She smiled to herself, wondering if her aunt ever threw anything away.

Janna pushed open the library door and scanned the room. Everything was just as she remembered it. She replaced the two books she had taken from the shelves and drew out three more. One at a time she blew the dust from their top edges. How long had it been since members of her family had turned these pages? She opened one book. "Copyright 1877."

After Janna had closed the library door she decided this wasn't so bad. It had reassured her to find the library just as she had seen it earlier, and she wanted to know that nothing had been changed in the remaining two rooms.

The next room is Myrtle's, thought Janna. She would say good morning to the headless dress form. She turned the knob. The door was locked. Hmmm, maybe she had remembered wrong. She walked down the hall to the fourth room, which opened to her touch. So she was right: The locked room *was* Myrtle's, for the unlocked room was the one with all the pictures.

Who was locking and unlocking the rooms, wondered Janna. But intrigued with the opportunity of inspecting the room, she decided it must be the work of Trebla.

The newly unlocked room was an art gallery, which undoubtedly had been a source of pride to her ancestors. Some of the paintings were oil portraits, some were country scenes. Janna stood for some time before the massive painting of Briar Rose Manor in its days of splendor. On the manicured lawn posed three young ladies in hoop skirts. On each side of the huge picture was a set of three smaller pictures. All were of the same size and all were in identical frames. To the right of the house picture were portraits of three bearded young men. To its left were three attractive but unsmiling young ladies, hair piled high on their heads. Janna wondered who they were.

In her decision to go upstairs, Janna had forgotten the baby rabbit. Now she remembered that she had a pet who was probably hungry. Babies need to be fed often, she knew. She would heat milk for her charge before she did anything else.

Carrying her books, she descended the stairs, choosing her steps carefully. She made hardly a sound.

When Janna reached her room she hurried to the rabbit's clover nest. She would feed him, then play with him. Soon he would know that he belonged to her. He'd come hopping when she called, and she'd have fun watching him twitch his nose in excitement when she offered him a special treat like a carrot. It would be good to have a pet. It would make her less lonely.

Bunny was not in the box. How could he have gotten out? She had thought he was too young to climb over the side. At least he couldn't have escaped from the room. The door had been closed all of the time she was gone.

Janna stooped to look under the dresser. Not there. Nor was he under the chair where she'd flung her pajamas. She looked in the dark corners of the closet. She wished he'd make a noise so that she would know where he was. She lay on the floor on her stomach to peer under the bed. Gray fuzz balls rested lightly on the layer of dust that covered the floor. Her apple core and napkin were there where she had left them the other night. Back in one shadowed corner was a tiny, brown huddled lump of fur.

"Come here, little rabbit," Janna called softly. The rabbit remained motionless.

"I guess I'll have to come to you."

Janna wiggled under the bed, propelled by her elbows. She bumped her head on the slats and ducked lower. Finally her hand closed over the rabbit. Its body was stiff and cold.

Involuntarily she jerked back her hand, suddenly squeamish about touching the animal she had petted the evening before.

"Oh, Bunny, you're dead! Poor little Bunny!" She studied it for a moment then she squirmed out from under the bed. She got a tissue from the box in her suitcase, then wormed her way again to the animal. Covering the rabbit, she carried him out. She laid him in the clover-filled box.

"You won't need any more milk, Bunny," she said sadly. "I'm still not going to let Prowler have you. I'm going to bury you properly as soon as I've eaten breakfast."

When she went to the kitchen she found that Trebla had already cooked the oatmeal and was sitting at the table, eating her share. Janna joined her.

Breakfast was a silent affair. Janna didn't want to tell Trebla about Bunny's death. Even if she had been only trying to acquaint Janna with the way of wild things, she might say I told you so. Janna didn't want to risk that.

As soon as breakfast was over and the dishes were washed, the two girls parted.

Janna returned to her room. She knew how to plan a funeral for a pet. She remembered several burials that she, Kerri, and Claude had conducted in their backyard. There had been a funeral when Kerri's chameleon had expired. And for Claude's curious yellow kitten after it had had the refrigerator door accidentally slammed on its head. And when Mother's canary died they had had a funeral even for it. Her bunny, too, must be buried decently.

First Janna needed a small box. She remembered seeing an empty matchbox in the kitchen. It would be just the right size. She would line it with something soft and pretty. The yellow tissues would be perfect. The little brown bunny would look just right in a soft yellow nest. She would need a piece of cardboard for a marker, too.

Janna went to the kitchen for the matchbox. *Where can I get material for a marker?* she wondered. Then she remembered that she had emptied the cracker box two nights before. She would cut a piece from it. But that took scissors and she had none. Somewhere she had seen a pair of scissors. She racked her brain. In the silverware drawer at the very back with the butcher knives. She pulled out the drawer. Her memory was right.

Taking the two boxes and the pair of scissors, Janna returned to her room. She lined the matchbox with tissues, then she laid the small rabbit inside. After she had closed the cardboard casket, she cut a rectangle from one side of the cracker box. Searching through her suitcase she found a pen. She sat on the edge of her bed, pasteboard rectangle resting on a book on her knees. She chewed her pen top, deep in thought. Then she wrote: "Bunny Edmundson, infant—Gone but not forgotten."

Pleased with her inscription, she took the matchbox coffin and the marker and went to the toolshed for a spade. She'd ask Mr. Hoskins if it would be all right for her to use the one she'd seen standing there in a corner.

She searched and called around the barn for the hired man, but he seemed not to have come to work. In answer to her voice, however, Prowler appeared. As she knelt to pet him, she noticed in the dust beside him a footprint of a man's cowboy boot. Had the mysterious intruder come again? It made her skin prickle to think that someone came and went so secretly that he was never seen. She was sure that he meant no good.

Janna decided, even though the permission to use it hadn't been given, that she would borrow the spade. She wouldn't hurt it, and she'd soon have it back leaning in the corner where she'd found it. She would go only as far as the edge of the trees, and she wouldn't stay long. The footprint reminded her of the two times she had seen a man disappear into the trees. She didn't relish the thought of going deeply into the dark, fearsome woods. However, she was sure that that had been the home of the baby rabbit, so it seemed right that she should bury him there.

As Janna left the shed she heard Mike call from the road.

"Coming!" she answered. She dropped the spade and, matchbox and marker still in her hand, hurried to the front gate.

"Ready to go?"

Did he sound eager, or was she imagining it?

"I had planned to, but I can't right now. Look." She slid open the matchbox and showed the rabbit inside.

"Prowler caught it. He gave it to me and I thought it would live, but it didn't."

Mike shook his head. "They usually don't."

Janna caught her breath sharply as Mike echoed Trebla. "Well, I'm going to bury it," she said shortly.

Mike looked at her, puzzled. "Okay. But I have to make my deliveries. It's a short run; I'll stop by when I'm through."

As Mike rode off, Janna returned to the shed for the spade. It was one thing to be irritated with Trebla, but quite another to be irritated with Mike. Janna was beginning to feel like a little girl for getting upset because no one seemed to share her feelings about the rabbit—in life or death.

Oh, well, she thought, *I planned to bury the rabbit and I will bury the rabbit.*

On the edge of the woods she saw something that lifted her heart: a ring of moss. She had heard that such moss rings were called fairy circles and were supposed to have been made by the dancing of the little people. She would bury Bunny in the fairy ring. Wild violets and sheep sorrel flowers dotted the ground with purple blossoms.

She dug a shallow hole and placed the box in it. She had planned to dig a deeper hole but when she hit rocks, she decided the hole was deep enough. She covered the box with dirt and sprinkled purple flowers over the top of the grave and placed the pasteboard marker at Bunny's head.

Just as Janna picked up the spade to leave, she heard a strange sound—not animal, not human. She listened more closely. Could it be singing? Or wailing? The tones rose and fell but there were no words. Then, a short distance farther into the trees she spied him. It was the same green-caped man she had seen stealing through the barn lot. It was he who was making the strange singing wail. And he dug into the earth as he sang. What was *he* preparing to bury?

94

9

The Ghost in the Fog

Janna dropped the spade and fled. She forgot everything in her panic to get out of the woods. She leaped over a fallen log and tore through a tangle of blackberry bushes. Her feet seemed to skim the ground as she ran. Finally she reached the barn. She sat down and leaned against its rough oak siding. Her legs were weak and her heart pounded so hard that she felt like a hollow drum vibrating to its beat.

Then she heard Mike call.

Not even taking time to answer, she jumped up and flew to the gate. "Oh, Mike! I'm so glad to see you! I've just had the awfullest scare!"

He was going to ask if it was a story the twins would like but he stopped short. "What happened to your legs?"

Janna looked down at the cuts and scratches on her legs in surprise. . . . "Some kind of bush, I guess— Oh, Mike, listen," she grabbed his arm, "I went to the woods to bury the bunny and I heard the scariest sound. A man was digging a hole and he was making this strange, weird noise, kinda like a wailing chant, only I couldn't understand any words."

"What did he look like?"

"I don't know. All I noticed was that he wore a green cape."

"That sounds like Kiah. He's weird, all right. I meet him now and then in the woods. He lives by himself in a little cabin. No one really knows him. He comes and goes as he chooses and seems to feel the whole country belongs to him. The police locked him up once for trespassing, but they soon let him go."

"Mike, I was so scared that I dropped the spade. Would you please come with me to get it?"

"Sure," said Mike, dropping the kickstand on his bike.

"Do you think Kiah would come into Aunt Agatha's house?" Janna asked as they walked slowly toward the woods.

Mike shrugged. "Hard to know. Has someone been in the house?"

"Well, I have heard footsteps in the upstairs rooms when I know Trebla was in her room."

"Could be the creaks of an old house," Mike said. "And this one is prehistoric."

Janna shook her head. "You wouldn't say that if you heard these noises. . . . Trebla says the house isn't friendly to strangers. Isn't that spooky?"

Mike laughed. "I guess it might be if you believe in ghosts."

"Don't laugh, Mike; one night I *did* see a ghost— or somebody who wanted me think it was a ghost— floating up the stairs. . . . Do you believe in ghosts?"

"Naw—there aren't any ghosts. I'll bet that there was a real live person wearing that sheet you saw."

"That's what I thought!" said Janna, obviously relieved. She laughed. "I can go up the stairs now without making a sound. You just walk near the wall instead of in the middle of the steps."

After a pause, Janna continued. "There are other

96

things, though. I've heard violin music when no one was here except me. And sometimes the rooms upstairs are locked and sometimes they're unlocked. And one day a strange man was prowling around the barn lot, and he ran away when I called to him. I didn't see his face but he left the print of a cowboy boot in the dust. Another time the green-cloaked man was sneaking around the barn."

"It sounds as if there's a mystery at your aunt's house."

They had almost reached the edge of the woods. Janna was glad that Mike was with her. And she was glad for his height. She felt herself looking up to him in more ways than one. An involuntary shiver shook her as she remembered the chanting of the green-cloaked man. Mike seemed to sense her mood. He reached for her hand and held it as they entered the woods.

"Do you ever see any footprints upstairs?"

"No, but I've never really looked. I'm not sure that the floors are dusty enough to show prints."

"Ride home with me after we get the shovel and I'll give you a can of plaster powder to sprinkle around upstairs. That will show us whether or not someone besides the Mitchell ghost roams around."

Janna enjoyed the extra time she had with Mike as she rode to his house. Mrs. Morris and Mike's sisters were glad to see her again, and they coaxed her into staying for lunch. Actually, she didn't need much coaxing. Grilled cheese sandwiches and a bowl of ham and beans sounded more appealing than her regular diet of eggs and blackberries.

Janna wanted to stay longer, but she had to get going so she could visit Aunt Agatha. She thanked

Mrs. Morris for the lunch and said good-bye to Mike and the twins.

When she reached Briar Rose Manor, Janna grabbed the can of plaster powder out of the basket and hurried to her room. After putting it on the top shelf of her closet, far back in the shadows, she could no longer ignore the gravel in her shoe and sat on the bed to remove it. Then she noticed the matchbox on the bed beside her. She picked it up curiously.

"This looks just like the one I buried Bunny in," she said aloud. "How did it get here?" She slid the top open, then dropped the box on the bed with a shriek of horror. Inside, on top of a piece of paper, lay two tiny rabbit ears. Bunny's ears! Taking care not to touch them, she drew out the paper. "Hear this," the crude printing read, "go away. You are not wanted here."

"What a cruel thing to do!" she said out loud.

Who could have done it? She was sure that Trebla wanted her gone. There was the hired man. He, too, seemed to want her to leave. But she hadn't seen either of them in the woods when she was there to bury Bunny. Kiah! Had he seen her? She shivered at the memory of his weird incantation. Why would he want her to leave Briar Rose Manor?

Her face became grim with determination. Angrily she tore the paper into pieces. She returned the bits to the matchbox and closed the lid. She was not going to be frightened away. Aunt Agatha needed her, and she belonged here.

She looked at the box with revulsion. How could anyone do anything so sick? She carried the box outside. She walked through the barn lot to a tall patch of wild sunflowers and threw the box as far as she could into the spreading thicket. A second burial.

No one should have to have a second burial, she thought.

As she returned to the house, her impatience to see Aunt Agatha crowded out her anger over the cruel warning. She breathed a prayer to God, asking Him to help her keep a level head and to decide later whether or not to confront Trebla about the bunny. She'd try to learn more about Mr. Hoskins, too, and Kiah. She put on a clean pair of jeans and got on her bike.

As Janna peddled toward Kay, she debated telling her aunt about the strange happenings at Briar Rose Manor. Then she became eager to talk to her aunt and hear more about the family that she had just discovered. Finally she decided that because of her aunt's physical condition she would not worry her with the mysteries at the house. Aunt Agatha needed to concentrate on getting well.

Besides, with Mike helping her now, perhaps she would be able to solve them without upsetting her.

At the hospital, Janna hurried to room 202, remembering the warm, happy welcome Aunt Agatha had given her the day before. Her aunt was probably even stronger today. Perhaps she'd be able to come back to Briar Rose Manor soon. Janna could take care of her there.

Eagerly Janna stepped into her aunt's hospital room. Aunt Agatha was not alone. She was being hugged by someone—Trebla, who had on a fresh top and her hair in two braids instead of a ponytail. But she still wore the watch with the ugly leather band, Janna noted. A rush of jealousy flooded her, and she found herself rebuilding a wall of dislike and distrust.

Then Janna realized that her aunt was crying and

that Trebla was comforting her. Janna stood still, uncertain about what to do.

"Aunt Agatha?" she said hesitantly.

Trebla drew back, and Aunt Agatha looked toward the door, dabbing a tissue at her eyes.

"Aunt Agatha, what's wrong?" Janna hurried to the bedside of her aunt.

"The doctor says that I'll never be able to live alone again. That it wouldn't be safe, that I couldn't take care of myself." She started to cry again, and Trebla patted her shoulder.

"I'll be here. I can take care of you." Janna spoke around the lump in her throat.

"But I don't have any money even to live on," Aunt Agatha moaned. "These hospital bills will take the rest of the money I have left. I'll have to go on welfare and go to a nursing home."

"Couldn't you sell all your land around the house? Wouldn't that be enough to pay the hospital? And maybe I could learn to do what Mr. Hoskins does, and you wouldn't have to pay me . . . "

"Honey," her aunt smiled warmly at Janna and shook her head slowly, "that's awfully sweet of you, but I'm afraid I owe much more than a hired man's salary. And actually I don't pay Andrew in money. He grazes his cows on my land and then does odd jobs for me in exchange."

She paused and wiped her nose. "As for selling some of Briar Rose, everything is mortgaged for more than it would sell for. I thought I wouldn't live long enough to use up my credit, but I can't borrow any more. The only thing I can do is sell everything, pay my debts, and go to a nursing home. I hate to take welfare." Aunt Agatha began to cry again. Janna stood by helplessly.

100

At last Aunt Agatha regained her composure.

"Janna, I'm afraid I need to ask a very big favor of you." Aunt Agatha reached her good hand out toward Janna.

Janna took her aunt's hand. Trebla watched, impassively.

"I'd like for you to sort through everything in the house and get it ready for sale. Perhaps Mrs. Morris will help you; she's very kind. And, of course, you can count on Trebla." She stifled a sob. "I want you to have any of the family mementos that you want; you decide what is to be sold—oh, if only I hadn't gotten sick!" She broke out again in sobs.

"It'll be all right," said Janna. "You know, my mother has always said that one of my strengths is that I can plan and organize things. I'll do my best for you, Aunt Agatha."

But she seemed not to hear. "I just can't leave Briar Rose Manor. I've spent all my life there."

Janna had never seen anyone cry with such hopelessness. She leaned over and hugged her aunt. The woman's sobbing quieted gradually until finally she lay red-eyed and spent on her pillow.

Janna spoke in a small, subdued voice, "You'll never be alone, Aunt Agatha. I'll do what you asked. Then we'll work something out."

"The Lord sent you at just the right time, dear," Aunt Agatha said patting Janna's arm. "You have been such a comfort to me."

Janna smiled. It was good to know she didn't come at a bad time after all, as both Trebla and Andy Hoskins had tried to make her believe.

The old woman began repeating herself. "I want you to keep for yourself anything that you want.

There isn't much to be sold, but it will all have to go. Oh, if only I hadn't gotten sick!"

Trebla spoke. "I'll go tell the banker you need to talk to him, Miss Agatha, but I'll be back later." She bent to kiss the old woman, then slipped from the room.

After Trebla had left, Aunt Agatha turned her attention to Janna. "I'm sorry things are working out so badly while you're here." She reached for another tissue and blew her nose. When she looked again at Janna, her eyes and nose were red but her mouth attempted a smile.

"I have something you will like to see," she said. She pointed to a box on the foot of the bed. "I had Trebla bring my old picture album so that I could show you some photographs of your ancestors and relatives."

"Oh, I'd love to see them!" Janna pushed her glasses up on her nose. "Do you have pictures of my parents?"

"Only the wedding picture they sent me and a few snapshots of your mother when she was a girl."

For an hour the two heads were bent over the pages of the old album. Finally, remembering that she had stayed past her aunt's strength on her last visit, Janna felt that she should leave.

As she peddled back to Briar Rose Manor, she was torn with two emotions. The happy part of her was eager to transcribe into her diary as much of Aunt Agatha's conversation as she could reconstruct. She was glad that she had taken notes; this time she wouldn't be dependent wholly on her memory. The sad part of her grieved for Aunt Agatha. She must find some way to save Briar Rose Manor for its owner.

Surely the old house held valuable antiques, which could be sold.

As soon as she reached her room she changed back into shorts. She decided to sprinkle the powder upstairs. She wanted to do this before Trebla came. Tomorrow she would make a thorough examination of everything in the house to see what could be sold.

She slipped upstairs with the can in her hand, carefully treading near the wall as she climbed. It had become a contest with herself; each time she tried to see how much quieter she could be.

She opened the door to the storeroom. Not much of its floor was exposed, but when she left, it was covered with a thin white film.

Janna went directly across the hall to the room she had labeled the picture gallery. For a few minutes she paused to admire the painting of Briar Rose Manor and the six handsome portraits that flanked it: bearded men on one side, lovely ladies on the other. Aunt Agatha had said that Janna could keep any items she wanted. Janna made a mental note to set aside the portraits. Then she scattered plaster powder evenly over the bare floor.

Down the hall, the next room was Myrtle's. Janna turned the doorknob to the room where the sheet-sheathed dress-form had lain on the couch. The door was still locked. Janna turned the knob again. No doubt about it, someone had been here and locked the door since day before yesterday.

In the library she began liberally sprinkling white dust on the floor. *Only a ghost could move around in here without leaving tracks now.* The cloud of powder tickled her nose until she sneezed.

As Janna returned to her room she encountered no one. Perhaps she wouldn't see Trebla until morning. She might have chores to do at her house. *Maybe her father doesn't like her helping out at someone else's house.* That was such a sudden and sympathetic thought about Trebla that Janna wondered where it came from.

She would have eggs again for supper. Probably they hadn't been gathered today. She was sure that there would be more than enough for a meal. She'd have canned blackberries, too. She sighed; this diet was beginning to get old.

The sun was setting as Janna started toward the henhouse. Dusk would soon swath the countryside in gray: the lonely time.

As Janna opened the gate to the barn lot, she saw something that she could hardly believe. At the far edge of the lot a ghostly figure drifted. A ghost in daylight! Janna remembered Mike's laugh when she talked of ghosts.

If it wasn't a spirit she was seeing, who was wearing that billowing sheet? And what were his reasons for wearing it?

Janna determined to follow him and try to find out. She was relieved when the figure made a sharp turn away from the darkening woods where she had seen the green-cloaked eccentric digging the mysterious hole.

The apparition sped along the trail. Sometimes he was hidden for a few minutes by a rise in the ground or by a tree. Janna didn't want to get close enough to be discovered. She attempted to dart from one hiding place to another. Now the specter had disappeared. There he was again. The trail had turned and the light had become so dim that the mysterious sheeted figure could easily lose itself from her sight. Janna wanted to follow him to his destination. If she could learn that, perhaps she could solve the secret of Aunt Agatha's house.

Wisps of fog were settling over the valley. The air was becoming misty white. The wraith-like form that moved before her could be seen only dimly now. Then it disappeared completely. Janna's eyes strained for a glimpse of the figure. Momentarily a breeze shifted the fog, and in the brief break before the whiteness enveloped it again, Janna saw the sheeted shape. At his side she saw something that she hadn't noticed before. Beside him hopped a dog—a small three-legged dog!

The fog was becoming more dense. Janna feared that she would be unable to find her way back to the house if she went any farther. Abandoning the chase, she retraced her steps. It was with relief that she saw looming before her the gray, mist-swathed bulk of the barn.

Janna entered the henhouse. The five hens had already settled for the night. As she felt in the dark nests for eggs, they sleepily clucked. She always reached fearfully into the nests at night. She had heard that snakes sometimes ate eggs. What if she touched a snake!

She found three eggs. Two she would boil for supper, leaving one for a sandwich for tomorrow's lunch. Eggs and oatmeal, oatmeal and eggs. Her stomach almost rebelled at the monotonous diet. When she went to town tomorrow she would buy something with flavor. Hot dogs, buns, a bottle of mustard, a jar of dill pickles, and a can of sauerkraut. She could make kraut dogs. Her mouth watered at the thought of it.

After she had eaten supper and cleaned the kitchen, Janna put the candle she had been using on the shelf in the hall, got the lamp from the kitchen, and went to her room. She'd write in her diary, write her daily letter home, then read from the books she'd brought downstairs.

As Janna recorded the events of the day in her diary, her pen could hardly keep up with her mind. Back at home she often wrote only a couple of lines a day. In the short time she'd been here she had half-filled the pink diary her father had given her at her last birthday. She realized, too, that she prayed much more here than she had at home. Then she'd been surrounded by Dad, Mother, and the children. Now that God was the only One she could turn to, she needed Him desperately. She was thankful that He was as close as her call.

She was adding this thought to her diary when she heard a sound from above. Someone was upstairs.

Since she knew that the ghost she had followed into the fog was most assuredly Mr. Hoskins, she knew she could count him out as the upstairs ghost—at least this time.

Who seems most unwilling to have me here? she asked herself. *Trebla.*

Janna could even imagine the reason for the other girl's hostility: She was jealous; she was fearful that Janna would replace her in Aunt Agatha's affection. That's why Trebla was trying to frighten her into leaving.

"Well, I won't leave, and I won't be afraid of her," she said resolutely as she got out of bed.

She would go upstairs and confront Trebla. She would assure her that she understood her affection for her Aunt Agatha, that between them maybe they could really help her. She would apologize for throwing the dishcloth at Trebla too. Perhaps, with God's help, Janna could turn an enemy into a friend. Perhaps if she and Trebla talked openly, their dislike for each other would disappear. "Lord, please let it work this way," she prayed aloud.

Janna felt it was necessary to catch Trebla in the act of something suspicious so she could not pretend being up to something else. Janna closed her door softly and stealthily climbed the steps into the dim light. The library door was closed; occasionally a light passed under the door. A flashlight. Suspicion arose again in Janna's mind. What was Trebla doing in that room? Had she another objective besides frightening her? Was she only pretending affection for Aunt Agatha?

Janna soundlessly moved to the closed door. She threw the door open and froze.

The figure standing before one of the bookshelves was not Trebla. It was a tall muscular man, and his face was covered with a ski mask. He seemed as startled as Janna was. His arms were filled with books drawn from one of the shelves. He dropped them with a crash and dashed to the closet, which was standing open.

Janna stared, dumbfounded (unconsciously wrinkling her nose), as he jerked the door shut after him. Was he as frightened as she was? Didn't he realize he was trapping himself? Did she dare open it?

10
Escape through the Closet

As questions raced through her mind, Janna heard a window being opened. Then she heard a thud on what she guessed was the back porch roof.

She tore open the door that the intruder had escaped through. She stared at the clothes in front of her and then noticed that the clothing on the right of the rack had been disturbed (and there was that smell again, faint but distinct). Ducking and groping along, she became more convinced of her direction when her feet became entagled in the heavy material of some garment that had fallen to the floor. She was feeling for a break in the surface of the wall, just as she had done the night she had entered her aunt's house for the first time. Very shortly she was rewarded with a door frame and a knob. However, when she turned the knob, the door would not yield. She realized the intruder had shoved something against the door. She had an idea what it was and where she would find the other side of the door. She quickly retraced her steps.

In the storeroom she found what she had suspected: Against the closet door was a stack of heavy boxes. Opposite was the window over the porch, wide open. *The library and the storeroom shared a walk-through closet.* Although she ran to the window, her hopes were small that she would see any more of the masked man. What greeted her reduced her hope to nothing. She had forgotten about the fog; between the fog and the darkness she couldn't even see the porch roof below.

She leaned against the wall, limp with shock. Her mouth was dry and her throat was still tight with an unuttered scream. Finally she latched the screen and lowered the window. Then she thought, *What good will this do? It didn't stop him before. He can come back.*

As Janna left the room, she remembered the plaster dust. At least now she would have footprints. Or rather, she would if her own hadn't blotted out all those made by the trespasser. She went downstairs to get the candle in the hall.

She searched the dusted floor. In several places the white dust marked the path of the intruder. She had seen them before—the masked man wore sharp-toed cowboy boots.

Satisfied with her identification, Janna went down the stairs as quickly as the candle would allow; squeaks and creaks accompanied her every step. Once inside her room, she leaned against the door and sighed.

After barring the door with the chair, she prepared for bed. Already she was wishing for daylight and sunshine.

She got into bed, wondering if she would sleep at all that night. Who was that masked man? It wasn't Andy Hoskins. Andy wore overalls and he didn't wear cowboy boots. Besides, this man was taller and younger. . . . He had had an armful of books. Surely he wasn't looking at them because he enjoyed reading . . . *And where is Trebla—but is she a part of this?*

Janna lay back on her pillow. *You've gotta get hold of yourself. Don't lose it. Remember the verses . . . Now I lay me down to sleep. I pray the Lord my soul to keep. If I should die*—Janna jerked herself upright. *Yuk!* She ran her hands through her short hair and shook it. She took a deep breath and lay back down. *The Lord . . . The Lord is . . . The Lord is . . . my light! The Lord is my light and my salvation— whom shall I fear? The Lord is the stronghold of my life—of whom shall I be afraid?—Psalm 27:1.*

With the comfort that Someone bigger than her— bigger even than the biggest prowler—was watching over her, she fell asleep.

When Janna awoke the next morning she blinked in surprise at the brightness in her room. She wondered why she had slept so late. Had she failed to hear her bird announcing the new day?

She dressed and then stepped outside the back door. She walked off the porch and turned toward the morning sun. She yawned and stretched; she rubbed her arms where the rays of the sun had penetrated.

Prowler came purring to her, declaring that it was a very good day indeed. She picked him up and snuggled him, stroking his head with her chin.

A light breeze tousled her hair, sunlight flashing through it, turning it an even lighter shade of blonde. The breeze also ruffled a small scattering of brown feathers on the ground where Prowler had been. Janna stared at the feathers for a moment, and then understanding burst upon her—Prowler had killed her phoebe! She dropped the cat.

"Prowler! How could you? You get enough to eat.

110

You don't need to kill birds!" Then she softened. "I shouldn't scold you, I guess. It's your nature to hunt. But I'm going to fix it so you won't kill any more birds. I'm going to get you a collar with bells on it when I go to town."

Janna heard Trebla rattling dishes in the kitchen. She had probably already cooked the oatmeal in the well house. Some morning, Janna decided, she would get up early enough to prepare this one meal that they shared. She would serve something different. Perhaps buttered toast and hot chocolate.

But her resolution of the night before, to make amends with Trebla, wavered. Should she tell Trebla of chasing the sheeted apparition into the fog? Or of her terrifying encounter with the masked intruder? Perhaps Trebla only pretended to be devoted to Aunt Agatha; her attitude could have been assumed only as a screen for actions not so innocent.

Janna decided to see what kind of response she got from Trebla first. She went into the kitchen, her mother's teaching about manners prompting a greeting.

"Mornin'," responded the girl seated at the table. "Oats are on the stove." From the odor hanging in the air Janna could tell that they had been scorched.

"Thanks," said Janna dryly. She scraped the oatmeal lightly from the pan, trying to leave the scorched coating. Trebla scooped the last bite from her bowl, pushed back her chair, and got up.

"You had a good night?" Trebla looked into Janna's face.

Janna stiffened involuntarily. "I slept okay. . . . Why?"

Trebla shrugged. "Just bein' polite. I guess I didn't wake you when I came in."

111

"I slept all right."

"Well, I gotta go. You'll be stayin' 'til you get done what your aunt wanted, I guess."

"Of course," replied Janna.

Trebla shook her head. "Just tryin' to be polite." With that she turned and left.

As Janna scrubbed out the oatmeal in the pan, she again tried to decide on Trebla's loyalties. *Does she really care about Aunt Agatha, and is she just jealous of me? Or is she showing her true self to me and just hiding it from Aunt Agatha? . . . But if so, why?*

Janna decided to forget the debate for the moment and treat Big Girl to some of the sugar cubes in the box she had noticed while putting away the dishes.

As she stepped outside, Prowler rose from his sunny spot, stretched lazily, and trotted to position himself two paces ahead of her. Tail held high, he marched as if he knew where she was going.

As she swung open the gate to the barn lot, she found her thoughts wandering to Andy Hoskins. She wondered what had been his destination through the fog last night.

The hired man was not in sight. She listened for the rattling of the feed bucket, which he often carried. There was no sound indicating the presence of Andy and his three-legged companion. She heard only the cackling of a hen and the horse's whinny.

"Hi, Big Girl," she called to the old mare.

The horse approached, then nuzzled in her outstretched hand for the bit of sugar. The bright sun made the gray flanks of the horse shine as if they were fine wood and had just been polished. The horse smell was pleasant in Janna's nostrils. When the sugar was gone, she stroked the horse's long nose.

112

"I wonder if you'd let me ride you sometime?" she asked.

Suddenly she had the disturbing feeling that she was being watched. Uneasily, she glanced over her shoulder toward the barn behind her. The hired man stood in the shadowed entrance. When he saw that he'd been noticed, he turned and disappeared into the darkness of the building.

"Janna!"

Janna whirled toward the sound of the voice. Mike was at the lot gate.

"How about riding with me this morning?" he asked.

Janna raced him to their bikes and then raced him to his first delivery.

"No more racing until after we finish the deliveries." He took two quarts out of his basket. "My customers are expecting milk, not butter," he said over his shoulder.

Janna nodded and then rested her arms on the handlebars and let her head hang forward. She was still in that position when Mike returned to his bike.

He placed a hand on Janna's neck and began a light massage. "Coach Williams teaches us techniques for getting tension out of each other. It's usually on legs though. . . . Does this help?"

"Ummmm," was all Janna said. Finally she raised her head and smiled, "You have a good coach."

They rode in silence for a while, listening to the whir of the tires on the asphalt. A small plane buzzed somewhere in the distance.

"Mike, my aunt is going to have to sell Briar Rose Manor."

"She is? Why?"

After Janna had explained, she shrugged her

shoulders and gave a little laugh. "Oh, well, Briar Rose Manor probably isn't safe for her anymore any way."

Mike looked over at Janna. "You mean because of her stroke and getting around on the steps and stairs?"

"Hmmm, I hadn't really even thought about that.... I was thinking of the strange things that have been going on, especially yesterday." She began with the bizarre behavior of the hired man, concluding with "... so do you have any idea what Mr. Hoskins was doing?"

"Nope. He's always been quiet. At least, he's never talked to me when I've been around him."

She hesitantly told him about the man she had surprised in the library. And about the footprints in the plaster powder.

"Sounds like your aunt's not the only one who might not be safe around her place." Janna noticed Mike's hands tighten and relax and then tighten again on the grips of his handlebars.

"Would you look at the footprints?" Janna asked.

"Uh, huh," was his only reply.

Janna wanted to reassure him with a touch or a word, but touching him while she was riding was out of the question, and she didn't think she could make any such words sound convincing.

When all the deliveries had been made, Mike and Janna peddled back to Briar Rose Manor. As they neared the house, Mike said, "Since we don't know about Trebla, maybe we should just act like I'm going to look at something in one of the rooms upstairs, the portraits or something."

"Okay, but I think she'll probably be gone. She usually just spends the night."

114

The house was empty and still. Its dark coolness chilled Janna. As soon as she held out her hand, Mike had it in his, giving it a gentle squeeze. The two went upstairs. The library was just as she had left it the night before.

Mike examined the prints on the floor, then followed them to the window. He raised the window, unhooked the screen, and climbed through. Janna watched as he walked to the edge of the porch roof.

Stepping into the walnut tree the phoebe had awakened Janna from each morning, Mike soon disappeared in its leafy branches. Janna followed to the edge of the roof. She watched him as he climbed back up the tree. As she stepped aside he moved easily back onto the roof.

"The tree's almost as good as a ladder," he said, shaking his head.

"But the screen?"

"Go inside and lock it."

Janna did so. Mike kneeled before the window and gave the bottom of the screen frame a sharp rap where the hook was attached.

Janna gasped. The hook, resting loosely in the catch of the window sill, had popped right out.

"If nothing's been done to them, these old houses are easy to get into. Windows are for keeping out the wind and rain; screens are for keeping out the insects. Even the doors are more for keeping out animals than people. Old people who've grown up around here don't even bother to lock up."

When he saw Janna's expression he added, "Course, they're liable to have a shotgun in the corner too. . . . Your aunt probably doesn't, though, huh?"

Janna bit her lip and shook her head.

They returned to the library. One by one they examined the books on the floor. They searched through the pages but found nothing unusual. Finally Janna returned them to the shelves. She sighed.

"We don't know much more than we did."

"At least you've seen the man who wears the boots. How big was he?"

"Taller than Mr. Hoskins. And he moved faster, too. I'm sure he was younger. He wore jeans, kind of tight . . . and definitely dirty, and a blue work shirt. . . . It was tucked into his pants . . . he wore one of those wide belts—you know, the kind that usually have a big buckle? But I didn't notice a big buckle."

"Hmm." Mike thought for a moment. "Can't think of who it might be."

"—And he smelled!" said Janna, wrinkling her nose.

" 'Smelled'?"

"You know, body odor, no bath."

Mike laughed. "Well, around here, not everyone's got indoor plumbing . . . or they're not used to it yet. So that clue may not count for much."

Janna laughed too, but it was because the thought had flashed through her mind that the intruder was lanky—like Mike—and she had dismissed the suspicion with, *No way, he would've had to been wearing clothes from the bottom of a laundry pile.*

"While you're up here, let me show you the other rooms," she said and led the way to the door. "You've already seen the storeroom, since that's where some of the tracks were." She led the way to the picture gallery.

"This is my favorite room upstairs," she said. "See the way Briar Rose Manor used to look?"

Mike surveyed the painting of the mansion. "Boy,

117

it doesn't look like that now!" He glanced around at the portraits. "Were all these your ancestors?"

"I think so."

Mike studied the portrait of the girl in the yellow dress. "She's the prettiest one," he decided. He turned to Janna. "Take off your glasses.... Now don't smile.... No, *don't* smile."

Janna laughed. "I can't help it. You're making me." She slapped him lightly on the shoulder.

"She looks a lot like you. But your smile would have helped her a whole lot."

Janna quickly put her glasses back in place; she could feel her neck reddening.

"What other rooms are up here?" Mike asked, heading for the door.

"One more," said Janna. "But it's locked." She turned the knob on Myrtle's room, and the door opened.

"Well, it *was* locked." She stepped inside and Mike followed. She turned to him. "I want you to meet a friend of mine—Myrtle."

She led him to the wall where the couch stood. It was empty. Myrtle was gone! Janna surveyed the room in astonishment. Myrtle now stood by the window, as if on vigil.

"Mike, she's been moved! He must have keys to the rooms."

"You should stay with us. Mom and Dad wouldn't mind at all. In fact, if they knew about this—"

"No. I'd never solve the mystery if I moved out, and I want to do it before Aunt Agatha gets out of the hospital. I don't want her to have to keep a a shotgun in the corner ... even if she might not be here much longer."

Mike and Janna walked back into the hallway.

"Mom doesn't think you're having much fun on your visit," he said. "She told me to tell you to come over if you get lonesome."

"I'm spending some time with Aunt Agatha. That's what I wanted. . . . And I enjoy being with you."

The Smile lit up his face. "Well . . . I don't think I'll tell Mom that last bit of information. She and the twins can tease to the point of orneriness."

As they walked down the stairs Mike looked at his watch. "I've got to go. I promised Mom I'd clean the garage today."

"And I promised Aunt Agatha that I would get things ready for the auction, and I want to visit her too."

Having made short work of lunch with a cold boiled egg, some raisins, and peanut butter and crackers, Janna peddled toward the hospital. She tried to block from her mind all of the depressing fears for the future. She tried as well to close the door on all the puzzling events of the past few days.

She was going to visit Aunt Agatha, her very own blood-relative. She would try to make their time together happy. She focused on the mix of wildflowers that topped the wrapping of old newspaper in the carrier of the bicycle (and thought ruefully of her attempt to handle the briar rose).

"Oh, Aunt Agatha, you're up—I mean your sitting in a chair!"

"Yes, I am, child, and look at this." She slowly raised her left arm from her lap and lowered it. "The feeling is coming back too."

She sat in the chair beside the bed, the gift shawl around her shoulders.

Janna looked about the room and almost skipped over to her aunt when she saw no other visitors.

119

"Oh and you've brought me some flowers! Thank you, honey. Why don't you just put them right here?" She motioned to the bedside stand beside her.

Janna bent to kiss the wrinkled cheek, noticing the faint, pleasant scent of honeysuckle.

"I'm glad you've come," said Aunt Agatha, smiling. "Now draw that chair close to me. I hope you are getting along all right." She patted Janna's arm. "Is Trebla taking good care of you?"

Janna forced a laugh. "Aunt Agatha, when I'm home—in Cincinnati—I often take care of three children. Fix dinner for the whole family. Do the wash . . . You don't need to worry about me taking care of myself."

Her aunt looked directly at her, her eyes narrowing; she started to say something, but then drew a breath and allowed her features to soften. "But I do worry. I certainly hadn't planned to be in the hospital when you were here. Your coming has brightened my days."

"I'm glad of that. I love being with you."

"Before we talk of anything else, I feel we must discuss some business," Aunt Agatha spoke hesitantly. "Even though the thought of selling Briar Rose Manor is like a horrible nightmare, I know that it must be done. I've talked with my banker and he says there's no other way. So I've had him arrange for the local auctioneer to conduct the sale. Colonel Clark, the auctioneer, will call on you tomorrow. I would like for you to show him through the house so that he can determine what is salable."

"Of course, Aunt Agatha. I'll show him what's there. But don't give up hope. I'm praying that your home won't have to be sold. I'm sure something will prevent it."

"God's ways aren't our ways, child," said the woman as she reached for the album lying on the table beside her bed. "We were going to look at more pictures, weren't we?"

Janna sat enthralled as Aunt Agatha told of the days of a proud family's prime. The old lady made dim-featured faces come to life. The girl learned the names and stories of the six young people whose pictures flanked the painting of the mansion. They were brothers and sisters and Briar Rose Manor had once been their home. All of them had been born in the old mansion and had lived there until they reached adulthood. Then they had married and scattered. Aunt Agatha's stories were so vivid that Janna felt that she, too, had known these people. Her family was taking shape before her eyes.

When the last page of the album had been inspected, Aunt Agatha laid it on the table.

"I have something else that I know will interest you." She reached for a bulky brown sack. "This is our family Bible."

From the sack she drew a worn book. Its cover was faded and shabby, and loose leaves extended raggedly from its edges. Aunt Agatha opened the Bible. Between the New Testament and the Old Testament was a lengthy, handwritten family register.

"You wrote of wishing for a geneology. Here it is."

"Oh, Aunt Agatha, a family tree! I didn't know one existed." Janna bent over the book lying on her aunt's lap. Now she could tell Brooke she had her own family tree. "Tell me about it!"

Twenty minutes later when Janna rose to go, her aunt handed her the album and the Bible.

"Take these to the house with you. You can look

121

at them more there. And something else—have you been in any of the upstairs rooms?"

Janna nodded.

"One of them is full of boxes and stacks of papers . . ."

The storeroom, Janna thought.

". . . There are two trunks there. They're so covered up that you may not have noticed them. Open them and look through them all you like. I want you to have the two trunks, the Bible, and the picture album for your own."

"Thank you, Aunt Agatha! You're being so sweet to me!" She bent over and hugged the lady.

"I love you, little niece." Aunt Agatha's eyes were filled with tears. "I had wanted to do much more for you than this, but I won't be able to."

Janna was optimistic as she left the hospital. Everything was going to work out all right, she was sure. It *had* to.

She had started home when she remembered that she had planned to do some shopping. Carefully wheeling the bike around so the album and the Bible wouldn't shift in the basket, Janna headed toward where she thought the main street would be. Finding a variety store, she bought a belled collar for Prowler. Then she went to a grocery store and purchased mustard, hot dogs, buns, dill pickles, and sauerkraut. *No egg sandwiches for me tonight.* Soon she was again cycling toward Briar Rose Manor.

As Janna entered the yard she heard the strains of violin music. She froze in her steps. The tune ended without her being able to tell where in the house— if it was in the house—it was coming from. All was

122

still. She stood motionless, waiting for it to resume. When it didn't, she slipped to her room. She felt as if she had been torn from the sunlight into the chill of a tomb.

11

The Puzzle of the Portraits

Janna pushed thoughts of the violin music from her mind. She had anticipated a delightful explo ration of the trunks in the room above; she was de termined that it should not be ruined. She placed the picture album and the sack containing the old Bible on the shelf in the top of her closet, then bounded upstairs to the storeroom.

However, when she saw the footprints on the floor her mind flew back to the frightening events of the night before. Then her arms stiffened at her side and her hands became fists. Wherever she saw the alien prints, she scuffed them out with her shoe.

At last she surveyed the room. Where were the trunks? There they were, under that pile of ragged quilts. Janna moved the quilts and pulled the two trunks into the middle of the floor. One was large one small; neither was locked.

She flipped open both lids. The trunks smelled of mothballs. The larger one held clothes; the small one, papers, letters, and books. Leaving the lids open she turned to the larger trunk.

She lifted out the article on top. It was a yellowed satin gown that had once been white, a wedding gown perhaps. Janna held it to her chin ... about her size. She'd try it on later. She dug deeper into

124

the trunk. It had been carefully packed. Many of the garments were wrapped in paper too soft with age to rustle. Janna was happy to see that the cloth seemed to have survived the years better than the paper had.

Before the dim full-length mirror that hung on the wall, Janna curtsied, swirled, and batted her eyes behind an imaginary fan. Two hours later she reached the bottom of the trunk. She repacked each piece just as she had found it.

Maybe some of these very gowns were worn by the ladies in the pictures beside the painting of Briar Rose Manor, thought Janna. Closing the clothing trunk, she decided to go to the art gallery and see if she recognized any of the dresses.

After she had carried the small trunk to the head of the stairs, she returned to the room where the portraits were. She remembered that the girl in the center was wearing a yellow dress much like the one that had almost fit her.

Janna opened the door and walked into the room. She stood before the three portraits for a moment, cocking her head one way and then the other; her face clouded into a frown. The girl in the center was wearing blue—but Janna was sure that she had been wearing yellow. Then she noticed that to the right of the girl in blue was the portrait of a bearded young man. She looked at the three pictures on the other side of the painting of the mansion. There, flanked on each side by one of her brothers, was her girl in yellow.

Oh, no—someone has rearranged the display!

For some reason, it was one thing to think the intruder had keys to the rooms, but quite another to see signs of his presence. Janna almost tripped over her own feet as she scuttled toward the door. Yanking it open she was at the head of the stairs in a single bound, again almost tripping, this time over the small trunk. She scrambled heedlessly down the stairs and out onto the front porch. She leaned on a support post and breathed in the fresh air. Insects were tuning up, twilight time. Janna shivered.

As she stared down at the worn porch steps, she remembered that she had sprinkled plaster dust over the floor of the picture gallery. She looked back at the door into the house. Were there footprints running along the wall where the pictures hung? Another shiver ran down her spine.

Slowly she pulled away from the porch post, walked into the house, and climbed the stairs.

As Janna searched the picture gallery floor for footprints, the only ones she found were hers and Mike's. After she had shown the pictures to Mike that morning, she had forgotten to sprinkle more plaster dust. Had they left too many footprints of their own for later ones to show up?

Then she saw them: along one wall where she and Mike had not walked, a trail of sharp-toed, high-heeled prints. In some places the impressions were blurred, but in others they were distinct. The masked intruder was the one who had mixed up the portraits.

Now that her question was answered, fright tried to take control; fear was raising goosebumps on her skin. Her breathing was growing shallow and her heart beat faster. She wanted to fly from the room, down the steps, and to her room, but she remembered the small trunk. She forced herself to the door; she hung just inside the door and then peered into the dusky hall. Was he there, waiting for her? The shadowed hall was empty.

126

She ran across the hall and picked up the trunk. She could not use her hands to balance herself going down the stairs. Instead, she tried keeping her shoulder in contact with the stairwell wall as she stepped gingerly off the landing.

Finally in the kitchen, she leaned against the cold stove, waiting for her heart to slow its painful thumping. She lighted a candle and put it in the hall. Then she took the trunk to her room.

Back in the kitchen, she began collecting food for supper. She would take no time to cook a hot dog; she wanted to reach the security of her room as soon as possible. She made a peanut butter sandwich. After spearing a pickle from the jar and grabbing an apple from the box under the cupboard, she started down the hall toward her room. Only in this one place did she feel safe. She knew that her future lay with Aunt Agatha, but she had no love for the austere old house.

In a quick memory-flash she saw her home in Cincinnati with her adoptive family. That house was always cheerful. It held laughter, happiness, love. Janna's longing for her mother and father, for Kerri, Claude, and Lisa, swept over her. How blind she had been not to realize what treasures had been hers when she shared that home! Though she had found the place where she belonged by blood, she was empty of joy. Coming to Briar Rose Manor wasn't at all what she'd expected.

When Janna reached her room she set down her plate of food and barred the door with the chair. After she had eaten in semi-darkness, she lighted the kerosene lamp.

As she opened the small trunk, her eagerness for exploring its contents returned. She set aside packets of old letters tied with faded ribbons. She skimmed through a scrapbook of yellowed newspaper clippings. "Miss Allie Johnston weds Edgar Jackson Davis," proclaimed one. Janna strained to read the date. *1896?* There was another old family Bible, worn even more than was the one Aunt Agatha had given her. Three diaries, bound alike, were tied together with string. There were several packets of pictures.

Janna dug to the bottom of the trunk, placing the items in a circle around her on the floor. She wanted to make a quick examination of everything before settling down to reading the papers, one by one.

When the trunk was empty, Janna surveyed the circle. What should she read first? The letters, she decided.

Each packet of letters was addressed to a different person, she discovered. Within a given packet, the letters had been arranged chronologically. Several of the bundles contained letters addressed to a Miss Kitty Williams. Janna wondered who she was and if they were related—she would read her letters first.

She read letter after letter until finally her eyes grew heavy and she caught herself dozing between pages. She yawned and gently folding the last letter, slipped it into its envelope. She sighed with satisfaction; she was beginning to know some of her ancestors intimately. And she still had the diaries, more letters, the newspaper clippings, and the Bible to examine. She planned to spend all of the next morning reading them.

Stiff from sitting so long, Janna rose and stretched, then flexed her knees. She repacked the trunk and got ready for bed. She blew out the lamp and was soon asleep.

When Janna next opened her eyes she was surprised to see her room bright with sunlight. As she swung her legs out of bed she realized that not a sound had awakened her during the night. While she dressed, she wondered if her sound sleep meant that nothing strange or mysterious had happened in the old house. Was it possible that the masked intruder had given up his search of the house, that he had decided to look elsewhere for whatever he was looking for?

On this note, Janna unbarred her door and entered the hall. Then she thought of her resolve to fix breakfast some morning instead of leaving it to Trebla. However, as she rummaged around in the kitchen for an ingredient that would offer some variety, through the window she saw Trebla coming from the well house. Oh, well, since she had washed the breakfast dishes each day perhaps that made things even. She'd treat her taste buds to a bowl of sauerkraut at noon. Her saliva flowed at the thought.

As Trebla entered the kitchen, Prowler darted in, bells tinkling. She looked down at the cat and then at Janna. "Your doin'?"

"So he won't catch birds."

"Another way of seein' after wild things, huh?" said Trebla. "And how well have you done with the rabbit, Miss Know-It-All?"

Janna looked down at the floor. *I won't cry and she won't get the best of me.* She raised her head to meet Trebla's gaze. "Do you really care?"

Trebla looked at Janna long and hard. She knew the question went beyond wild things. Suddenly her body relaxed and she lowered her gaze. She then set the pan of oatmeal down on the table and quietly walked out.

Janna's eyes followed Trebla's retreat. Slowly she

sat down. She stared at the pan of oatmeal; Trebla had left without eating.

For a time Janna toyed with a spoon on the table. Finally she noticed the meowing of Prowler and poured him some milk. Then Janna ate. In the middle of breakfast cleanup she thought of her unfinished examination of the small trunk and quickened her pace. Then she headed back to her room.

She was copying geneological information from the old Bibles when she heard Mike call. She hurried to the front door and out onto the porch. Mike was at the gate.

"How was your night?"

"The best ever!"

His face broke into a grin. "Well, then, let's go."

"Not this time," Janna answered. "Stop by when you're through, though, okay?"

"Okay!" Mike echoed and peddled off. Janna returned to her room. An hour later Mike was at the door.

"So last night was a good night?"

"It really was," said Janna quickly as she opened the door for him. "And my Aunt Agatha is better: She can lift her arm some and feeling is coming back—come here, I want to show you something." She led him to her room. The floor was strewn with papers. The little open trunk sat in the middle of them.

"Aunt Agatha told me to look in her old trunks and I'm having more fun! Some of these letters are over a hundred years old. There are lots of pictures, too."

"You are feeling pretty good, aren't you?" Mike said, smiling.

"Yes, and I've been thinking. Since the guy in the

130

cowboy boots didn't find anything in the picture room yesterday—"

"What! The guy was here again!" Mike was wide-eyed and his mouth hung open.

Janna quickly explained, "When I came back from the hospital I found footprints in the room upstairs with the pictures. But that's what I wanted to tell you. I was thinking that since he didn't find anything, he's given up and that's why he didn't come back last night."

Janna looked into Mike's face for support for her conjecture. "Or maybe he did find something—how would we know?—the thing is, he didn't come back last night," she concluded lamely. She was carrying on like Brooke.

"Janna, what if you just didn't hear anything because of how hard you slept?" Mike asked the question quietly.

"Well, he could give up sometime, couldn't he?"

Mike looked at the piles of papers arranged around the small trunk. He looked at the dresser shoved against the window onto the porch. He rubbed his hand nervously on his hip.

"Yeah, he could. . . . Can I see the tracks?"

Janna sighed. "Sure."

The two went upstairs. Mike looked at the footprints, and Janna explained to him the changed positions of the portraits. One by one he lifted the pictures. Dust lay along the tops of the frames and spider webs made films over the backs. Mike examined the wall behind each.

"What are you looking for?"

"A secret opening. Help me with the picture of the house."

Together they lifted down the painting. The wall

131

behind it seemed smooth. Janna watched as Mike felt over every inch of the space in search of an irregularity.

"Nothing here except dust," he finally announced. He wiped his hands on his jeans.

"I never thought to look behind the pictures," said Janna.

"They don't have TV in Cincinnati? That's where the wall safes always are."

Janna stepped on his toe.

"Ouch," he laughed. Then he grew serious. "I hope you're right about this guy not coming back."

"It would be one less thing I'd have to worry about." Janna took a swipe at the dust on one of the picture frames. "My aunt plans to sell Briar Rose, but I know it hurts her; this is all the home she knows. If only we could solve this mystery I think we would know how to help her. But I'm completely in the dark. It's like trying to put together a jigsaw puzzle when half the pieces are missing. So I'm praying a lot."

"Do you think that might really help?" asked Mike, leaning against the wall.

"Well, it's helped me stay here. My aunt may like this place, but it gives me the creeps."

"You haven't been treated to the best tradition of Ozarks' hospitality here."

"That's another thing I've been able to pray about. You know my troubles with Trebla. I think my attitude toward her is better than it was."

Mike snorted and stood up straight. "Hey, it seems like she's the one who ought to be praying."

"But I'm the one who calls myself a Christian."

"What do you mean by that?"

Janna thought for a minute. "I mean that Jesus is my Savior and my Friend. God is my Father and

His Spirit helps me to live as I should. I want to do what will please Him." Janna hesitated and then went on. "I make mistakes and have hard times. I lose my temper. But when I come to God and admit my wrongs, He forgives me and gives me the strength to go on from there."

Mike grinned. "I guess I really know about all that. My folks have taken me to church practically every Sunday since I was two weeks old—say, I almost forgot—Mom wanted me to ask if you'd like to go to church with us tomorrow, then eat dinner with us. We could do something fun afterwards. You know, forget this place for a while."

Janna's disappointment in the new direction of their conversation showed only slightly, but Mike continued, ". . . and you could tell me more why you take being a Christian so seriously."

"Thanks. I'd like to. And I had been wondering where Aunt Agatha goes to church and where I would go. So now I know where I'll go." She smiled. ". . . Do you know where Aunt Agatha goes?"

"With us."

"I'm glad you take her. And thanks for asking me."

"We'll pick you up at nine."

Mike had been gone less than ten minutes when Janna heard a knock at the front door. When she answered it, a short, stocky man stood at the threshold. He was dressed in a tan, western-cut suit and shiny brown cowboy boots. He removed his Stetson hat with a flourish, revealing a shiny head.

"You must be Miss Janna. I'm Colonel Clark. Your aunt wants me to handle her sale next Tuesday, and I need to know what she has before I write up the sale bill."

"Come in. I've been expecting you."

The auctioneer entered, hat in hand.

"Let's start with the rooms upstairs and work our way back to the parlor," suggested Janna. She led the way. "This house is so old that I'm hoping you'll find lots of valuable antiques." *Then my prayers will be answered,* she thought.

"It's possible," said the auctioneer. "When a house stays in the possession of one family for generations, the contents can become valuable just because of their age. We'll see."

Janna dismissed the storage room as the first room to show. "There are four rooms up here. This one at the end of the hall is the library." Janna opened the door. "There must be hundreds of books and some of them are very old." The room smelled of musty paper, despite the number of times it had been opened since her coming.

The auctioneer stood before the dust-dimmed shelves. He pulled out a book and flipped it open. A silver fish darted from the pages and disappeared. He examined the book, then pulled out another. When he returned it to the shelf, he moved down a few feet and leaned close to read a faded title. He ran his finger over the cracked binding of a brown volume. Then he turned to Janna. "None of these look like collector's items. They're not in very good condition. I'll list them, but they probably won't bring much."

He turned to tap exploringly on the big desk. He attempted to open the long center drawer. It stuck. By working at it with short jerks, he finally got it open. It held a miscellany: pencil stubs, rubber bands rotten with age, rusty paper clips. One after another he pulled out the drawers. Some hung so tightly that he had to tug to open them. One was coming apart. Several were filled with papers.

"Have you looked through these old papers? I know a man who found over half a million dollars worth of bonds in an old desk that had belonged to his grandfather."

Janna's eyes lighted up. "I'll take them to Aunt Agatha. She should be the one to go through them."

Brushing the dust off his hands, the auctioneer said, "This old desk won't bring much. Have you noticed the peeling veneer on the sides?"

Janna silently nodded and led Colonel Clark across the hall.

"This room has furniture in it." But as Janna tried the door, she found it was still locked. Not wanting to mention the mysterious door-locker, she said, "Ooh, my aunt gave me a key to her room, but not this one."

"Let me see the key."

The colonel stuck it in the old lock on the door, jiggling it for a moment, and then turned it. "All the old locks in the house are probably the same, or very similar," he explained, handing the key back to Janna.

Recalling Mike's demonstration and "lecture" about the security of old houses, Janna found she wasn't surprised. She continued, "I don't know exactly what's in here."

Together Janna and the auctioneer removed the sheets that concealed the pieces of furniture. Stirred dust particles danced in the ray of sunlight streaming through the window. They tickled Janna's nose. Evidently Colonel Clark was also affected, for he whipped a blue bandana from his hip pocket and covered his face barely in time to muffle a giant sneeze.

"Pardon me!" he exclaimed, wiping his wet eyes. "Now let's see what we have here."

Janna watched as he examined the pitiful display that they had exposed: a dresser with a cracked mirror and a missing drawer; a worn green stuffed chair, leaning because of a broken leg; a davenport whose floral cover, once cheerful, had aged into depressing drabness. The couch that had been Myrtle's bed was worn out. Seams had split and gray stuffing oozed in two places. There were three unmatched kitchen chairs, each wobbly because of missing rungs.

Janna led the man back down the hall and opened the door of the picture gallery. The auctioneer stood before the painting of Briar Rose Manor.

"It's sad to see these old mansions run down. My daddy remembers when this house was a showplace." He looked around the room. "Those ornate old picture frames might bring a good price. The pictures wouldn't add to their value. You could keep them. They'd mean more to you or to Miss Agatha than they would to anyone else. Can you clean the frames by Tuesday?" He took a small book from his pocket and made a note of the number of paintings in the room.

Janna nodded numbly. Perhaps her prayers were not to be answered. Perhaps everything would be sold for a pittance and Aunt Agatha would have to go to a nursing home. Tuesday was so near.

Then her spirits rose a little. If the papers from the desk could be valuable, then maybe the storage room had promise, after all. Then there were the rooms downstairs.

However, after a quick survey of the storage room, Colonel Clark said, "If old magazines and newspapers were diamonds, lots of elderly people would be millionaires. Is there anything more up here?"

A lump in Janna's throat hurt so that she could hardly answer. She shook her head silently, then turned to precede the auctioneer down the squeaky steps.

First she opened the door to her bedroom.

"That bed is old enough to be salable," commented Colonel Clark. "Someone might want it for the iron head and foot." He glanced around the rest of the room. "I'd guess the chair might bring two dollars and the dresser and the desk each ten. No more." He turned to leave the room.

Across the hall was Aunt Agatha's room. The lock resisted her, but imitating the colonel's actions upstairs, she was finally able to turn the key and swing open the door. Aunt Agatha's room was almost as bare as her own. Its only ornaments were two portraits hanging on the wall, probably Aunt Agatha's parents. They were not the same couple on the parlor wall.

"This bed matches the one in the other room. It would sell. Those two picture frames, too." He added these to his list.

Janna led him to the kitchen. She knew already that he would find nothing of interest there. The dishes were mismatched. Many of them cracked or chipped. The pans were warped and bent, showing years of use.

A flicker of hope revived as they proceeded to the parlor. The auctioneer went immediately to stand before the grandfather clock. As if to greet him, the timepiece bonged twelve slow musical notes. In silence they listened and counted. The deep, somber tones hung in the air.

The auctioneer rubbed his hand over the smooth shiny case.

"Walnut," he said. "I'm a clock collector myself and this is a beauty. Must be well over a hundred years old." He got out his notebook and scribbled a few words. Then his eyes scanned the rest of the room. He sauntered to the organ.

"Does it work?"

Janna pulled out three of the stops, pumped vigorously, then with one finger picked out "Jesus Loves Me." The organ wheezed and gasped. It probably hadn't been played in years. Dust rose from its bellows and the auctioneer jerked his blue bandana from his pocket.

"A-a-choo!" he exploded. He wiped his eyes and returned his bandana to his pocket.

"It needs a lot of work done on it," he judged. "But some people collect them. It would sell." Again he pulled out his book. "Two more picture frames and a claw-footed table," he noted and scribbled this down.

Again he surveyed the room. "Not much more of value here."

Janna's heart sank. "The house should bring quite a bit, shouldn't it?"

"If it were in good shape, yes. But it would take too much to restore it. Why, it isn't even modern: no electricity, no indoor plumbing. Money's tight, too. It's a shame, but I doubt if it will sell for much. Used to be quite a showplace, too," he repeated. "What's outside?"

Janna led him to the barn. He poked around in each of the buildings. He stopped to examine the old buggy. "This should bring a fair price. It's in good condition, too."

He affectionately slapped the flank of the horse. "She doesn't have many years left in her."

He stuck his head in the henhouse. "How many hens?"

"Five." Janna watched him record the number in his book.

She felt as if she were plodding, step by step, toward a precipice and that there was no turning back. Tuesday was the deadline and it was only three days off. Something must be done before then.

Telling Janna he would be by the day before the sale, the auctioneer left. In the kitchen Janna contemplated the can of kraut that sat on the shelf, but she didn't think she could enjoy it. She would get another hamburger in town when she went to see Aunt Agatha.

She must empty the desk drawers and take the papers for Aunt Agatha's perusal. Momentarily a hope flickered. Maybe these papers would be the means of answering her prayers and through them Briar Rose Manor would be saved. She found a paper grocery sack and emptied the drawers into it.

12
Trapped

As Janna bicycled toward town she determined to make today's visit as pleasant as she could. She would tell Aunt Agatha only briefly of the visit of the auctioneer; then she would describe the fun she'd had in trying on the gowns in the trunk. Perhaps as a girl Aunt Agatha had worn some of them. And perhaps her own mother had played dress up with those same garments. Aunt Agatha would also need to sort the sackful of papers.

After lunch at the Snak Shack, Janna went to the hospital. She bounded up the stairs to the second floor.

Aunt Agatha was sitting in the chair by the bed. She was wearing the shawl that Janna had brought, and Trebla was brushing her thin gray hair. Janna watched the girl with mixed emotions: envy, sympathy, suspicion. Didn't Aunt Agatha realize the kind of person Trebla was?

Aunt Agatha spied Janna first, regarding her for a moment before she called, "Come in, Janna." She held out her hand to Janna. "Trebla wanted to pretty me up."

Trebla acknowledged Janna's presence with an expression of . . . what? contentment? smugness? self-satisfaction?

"This is a lovely shawl, dear," continued Aunt Agatha, "I must write to thank your mother for it."

"She enjoyed making it for you." Janna put the sack of papers on the bed. *I wonder how long Trebla plans to stay. If she stays, I can't. I can't really visit with Aunt Agatha when she's here.*

"Did the auctioneer come?" asked Aunt Agatha, a note of resignation in her voice.

"Yes. I showed him through the house and the barn. He took notes and said that he'd print the bills and distribute them. He'll be back Monday to make a final check on things."

"I won't be able to be at the sale," said Aunt Agatha. "I don't want to be there, anyway. Mr. Jones, the banker, will send a clerk to handle the money. Trebla will help you, of course." Aunt Agatha patted the girl's hand. Janna controlled herself, as envy and suspicion exercised inside her.

Janna gestured toward the sack of papers. "I found these in the desk upstairs. The auctioneer said he knew a man that found more than half a million dollars in bonds in some papers left by his grandfather." But it was hard for her to exchange her negative emotions for enthusiasm.

"I doubt if there's anything of value in them," said Aunt Agatha. Janna put the sack on the table that sat between her aunt and the bed. Piece by piece Aunt Agatha examined the sack's contents, and piece by piece set it aside, finally returning everything to the grocery sack.

"Burn it all," she told Janna. "There's nothing worth keeping."

After this disappointment Janna realized how much she had been counting on the papers to save

142

Briar Rose Manor. She felt as if a stone had settled in the pit of her stomach.

Conversation lagged. Janna refused to talk of her delight in the family mementos in the presence of Trebla . . . who gave no indication of leaving. So Janna rose.

"I need to do some sorting and preparing for the sale, so I think I'll go now." She kissed Aunt Agatha and plodded from the room.

Janna left a crooked trail on the dusty road as she pedaled toward home. Tears blinded her eyes because of her disappointment in her visit with Aunt Agatha and despondency over her aunt's grief at having to leave Briar Rose Manor.

The auctioneer had given little hope that the old estate would sell for enough even to pay the accumulated debts. Now the papers that had been in the desk were worthless. . . . If only she were rich she would buy Briar Rose Manor and then give it back to Aunt Agatha. She wanted to stop beside the road and cry for her aunt the way Baby Lisa did for anyone who was hurt.

When Janna stepped inside her room she stopped abruptly, then stiffened. Hadn't she put the trunk in the closet? She knew she had meant to. It was beside her bed. She opened the lid. She didn't remember the Bible being on top of everything else, but there it was. Had papers slipped off it when she moved the trunk?

Had someone searched her room? Trebla? Janna chided herself for always thinking of Trebla when she suspected something. Trebla was at the hospital when Janna got there and she was still there when Janna left. The masked intruder? She pulled her suitcases from under the bed and opened them. They had not been disturbed. *Dear Lord, help me to get it together. Aunt Agatha needs me.*

Janna dreaded the task she had assumed. It meant bringing about the destruction of generations of memories. But it must be done, and she had promised.

She knew that even the things not salable must be disposed of before a new owner could move in. She would list all the items that she was sure would not sell; then she would ask Mrs. Morris's advice about them.

With dragging feet she started upstairs. She would follow the same order she had with the auctioneer.

The first entry she made on her paper was "books." Undoubtedly there would be some unsold after Tuesday. The magazines, too, and the newspapers would be left. She hoped that either in Mineville or in Kay the Boy Scouts were having a paper drive.

Janna feared that no one would want the odds and ends that Aunt Agatha had collected over the years. She sighed at the thought of the storeroom. Though she had no affection for the gloomy old house, her heart was sad because of her love for its distressed owner. Even after Briar Rose Manor was sold Janna was determined to stay near Aunt Agatha, who would need her more than ever. She could spend much time with her in the nursing home. Janna's natural parents had left insurance for her own care and she was sure that her adoptive parents would allow her to use the money to live here.

At the thought of her Ohio family, tears swam in her eyes. Such a short time ago she had been blessed beyond measure—and she hadn't realized it. Now she felt that she would never feel joy again. Only her sense of duty moved her. Whatever the cost, she wouldn't desert her aunt.

Still following the route over which she had led the auctioneer, Janna stepped outside. She walked slowly toward the barn. The late afternoon sun stretched a long shadow before her. Prowler marched beside her, bells tinkling.

The auctioneer had noted the horse, the hens, and the buggy, but nothing else. Janna decided to see how much feed was in the barn. It could be sold; a dollar was a dollar. She entered the dusky barn. In the left-hand feed room she found three bales of hay, half a sack of corn, a tub of ground feed, and a sack of chicken feed. She wrote down these items, then went to the next enclosure. She raised the metal bar that secured the door to the small, dimly lighted room. The bin smelled of mice, but it was empty except for a dusty pile of loose hay. She and Prowler returned to the house.

As Janna ate her solitary supper, her mind searched feverishly for a solution to Aunt Agatha's problem. Saturday was gone. Three more sunrises and the day of the sale would be upon her.

When she went to her room, she was still struggling to find some way out of the dilemma. But whichever way she faced, the central fact remained—not enough money. The only way she could help her aunt was by taking as much of the burden of the sale as possible.

Finally, Janna barricaded her door and went to bed early. With the dresser in front of the window onto the porch, she no longer felt as vulnerable as she once had. She slept fitfully, troubled by dreams of her aunt's losing Briar Rose, of being chased, of not seeing the Edmundsons again. Around 10 o'clock she was awakened. At first she thought she had heard screaming, but then she decided it was her own dream that had contained the screaming. Finally she fell into a quiet, restful sleep.

Hours later she was wakened by a faint tapping. Instantly she was alert. She listened intently. The tapping seemed to come from upstairs, but not directly over her. She glanced at the clock. Its luminous dial glowed faintly in the dark. Two-fifteen.

She slipped on her jeans, pulled on a top, and, putting her glasses in place, moved the chair from her door. She would creep upstairs as noiselessly as a ghost and, after she had discovered what was making the noise, she would decide what to do.

She turned the knob, intending to give a gentle push. The door refused to open. She pushed harder. It seemed to be stuck at the top. Perplexed, she tried again, pushing with more force. Although there was give at the bottom of the door, there was none at the top. It was held in place in some way.

Whether it was stuck or locked, Janna was uncertain. She was beginning to distrust her conclusions as well as her memory. She would climb out the window. She moved the dresser as quietly as she could, then raised the window sash, inching it up a little at a time in an effort to do so noiselessly. Finally it was high enough for her to climb through. But when she unhooked the screen and pushed against it, it held in place. Only then did she accept the thought she had dreaded: Someone had sealed her exits—she was a prisoner!

Perspiration broke out on her skin and she began to shake. Her ears roared and her heart raced. She must get out! She would batter down the door. Then caution warned of the noise that that would make, and she fought for calm so she could think of a way to escape. She would cut the screen. That could be done quietly.

But how could she do that? A knife? Scissors? Had she returned the scissors she had used to make Bunny a grave marker?

She rummaged in the dark through the stack of papers on the dresser. The scissors were there!

Using them, Janna slashed the screen from top to bottom. A couple of horizontal gashes and she had made a hole large enough to climb through. She laid the scissors on the floor and pushed through the cut screen. Dozens of fine, sharp wires caught her hair, scratched her arms, and snagged her top and jeans. Finally she was outside on the porch. It was deep in shadow from the moon, only faintly obscured by a thin cloud covering.

She stood silent for a moment, listening. Two owls were carrying on a conversation. A distant dog barked, then barked again at its echo. She could hear nothing from the upper story of the house. She walked cautiously along the porch to the back door. If Trebla had left it unlocked after she came in—which she sometimes did (Janna thought it was just to worry her)—Janna would be able to get back into the house. It was locked. Janna laughed grimly to herself: Trebla just couldn't please her.

She stood for a moment at the door. She would get in through her aunt's bedroom. . . . No, her door was locked.

Walking quietly to the porch steps, she eyed the tree at the corner of the house. It would help if she knew which room the intruder was in. She was pretty certain the tapping hadn't come from above her bedroom, so she eliminated the storeroom. She decided to circle the house and see if she could see light from any of the upstairs windows.

But as Janna stepped off the porch, she was startled by a thump and the sudden jingle of bells, as Prowler dropped into sight. "Oh, Prowler, not tonight!" she whispered. She turned him around and pushed him in the opposite direction. "Go!"

As she had suspected, the intruder was at the front of the house, in the room with the draped furniture. So she could climb the tree at the back of the house and—*What am I doing going back in the house. Whoever it is will have to come back out. It's just a matter of time . . . and place.*

For a time Janna stood in the front yard, watching the intruder's light play across the shade. Suddenly she turned and ran to the front gate. Quietly she opened it and scooped up some gravel from the road. Returning to a spot just beneath the window, she began to pelt it with two or three of the small stones at a time.

The light disappeared. But was it turned off or taken from the room?

Janna backed away from the house and ran across the front yard to the opposite corner of the house. Which door—or window—would he come from? And if he chose to come out quietly . . . she could see only two of the house's three doors at a time. She was betting on the rear window and the "tree-ladder," but she wanted to keep the front door in view because if he came down the stairs, he could come directly out the front door.

She thought she heard something from the back of the house. Was the wind moving the branches of the tree or was there someone in it?

Suddenly a yowl split the air—Prowler!—followed

immediately by a yell, the swish and crack of limbs, and a thud and "Umph!"

Wanting to keep her distance from the intruder, Janna started toward the back of the house at a trot. But she was met by the jingle of bells and the flying form of Prowler. She hesitated, looking after his retreat and wondering if he was hurt. When she got to the back of the house, she could make out nothing in the shadow of the tree. But the tree itself presented a new silhouette: on one side a lower branch angled sharply toward the ground, throwing off the tree's symmetry.

Janna glanced about for the person she was pursuing. Dimly, through the moonlight, she could see a tall form—the man with the cowboy boots, she was sure—disappear into the long shadow of the barn. Was he limping?

Janna broke into a run. She slowed when she reached the shadow of the barn. Would she wait him out here? Had he trapped himself? But she had thought that when he had ducked into the closet the other night.

She stepped cautiously into the dark entrance; at the same time, a small but powerful beam of light struck her in the face. Startled and temporarily blinded, she turned toward what she thought was the entrance of the barn, only to run into a powerful grip and an almost equally powerful smell: She gasped as she grappled with the man. When her foot came down on top of his, he yelled in pain, dropping his flashlight and loosening his grip on Janna. (She stifled the impulse to say excuse me.)

Twisting free and giving the light a frantic kick (which put it out, if nothing else), Janna found herself plunging deeper into the barn as she fled from her adversary. She found the ladder to the loft, something familiar, and without thinking, she scrambled up it.

When she reached the top of the ladder, she had half formed a plan to use in some way the two bales she had seen in her investigation of the loft; perhaps she could use them to block her pursuer's ascent . . . or to drop on top of him.

She climbed into the dark loft. Here and there a moonbeam pierced the blackness. *The bales should be directly in front of me.* She was elated when she shuffled into them.

She had no idea of whether her attacker had pursued her or fled, but she was losing no time getting the bales of hay into place above the ladder. She tried to push them both at the same time. But they were either too heavy or caught on something. She decided she would then kneel on top of the one and push the other one away from it and toward the ladder.

When she mounted the first bale, it sagged slightly under her knees; she thought little of it. She was grateful for the jeans on her legs, but she wished for gloves as she poked and pushed at the second bale.

Suddenly the bale under her sagged, shifted, and broke; for a moment she felt herself being wedged, sandwich-like, between its two halves. Then everything seemed to give way and she fell in the darkness. She landed on all fours in a pile of loose hay and crumpled into a heap. Stunned, she lay on her side for a time. Then slowly she rolled onto her back and opened her eyes.

She could make out a ragged hole far above her. *Must have been . . . a trapdoor,* she thought. She tried raising her arms and working her hands. They seemed all right. She sat up with relative ease, but one knee was tender. Slowly another thought formed, *Is it blacker in front of me than it is behind me?*

She struggled about awkwardly on the hay, edging onto some kind of coarse material. She was trying to picture the things she was feeling, but a painful twinge in her right knee distracted her. Gingerly she made it to her feet and turned around. Facing a narrow, angular entrance of pale darkness, Janna realized she was squinting and attempted to push her glasses up on her nose to bring the fuzzy lines into focus—she was without her glasses!

Then she became conscious of sounds. She held her breath to listen. He was still out there! And he was coming! Above the pounding of her heart she could hear the uneven clumping of boots, an occasional grunt of pain, and finally the ragged breathing, as the man approached her hiding place.

Oh, God, help me! She was almost sure the barn wall would be behind her. Hoping to find an exit away from her approaching attacker, she turned to her right and put out her hands, stumbling over the piles of hay and other material beneath her feet. At the same time that her hands touched the rough wood wall, she realized where she was—in the corn bin. There was no other exit!

And then she remembered her dream, the dream she had had the night before she left on her trip: being pursued, falling, the darkness, her fear. Now Janna was terrified. It was a nightmare come true.

She wished desperately that she were safely back within her room. This man—whose identity was doubly hidden, by darkness and a mask—must have some malicious purpose for his actions. Obviously he didn't want her to find the answer to the mystery of

Briar Rose Manor. Janna's mouth was dry and her heart was pounding.

The man had halted just outside the door. What was he going to do! Janna felt that her head would burst with the tension of terror. He did not speak, but she could still hear his breathing. It was more regular now. She prayed that the wild thumping of her heart would not reveal where she was pressed against the wall.

What was he waiting for? Suddenly the door slammed shut—he wasn't coming in after her! There were some indistinguishable sounds, including the protest of a rusty hinge and a final satisfied grunt. Then the irregular sound of footsteps told Janna he was limping away.

Janna leaned against the wall in relief, and then wonder, and then . . . the slow grasp of fear. Hands outstretched, she stumbled in the direction of the door. One hand touched the wall and the other the door. There was hardly a crack between the door and its frame. She felt over the door with both hands. It was solid. She was locked in the darkness.

She began to shake. Even her teeth chattered. She began crying. If only her mother were here to comfort her, as she had been after the nightmare. But this was no nightmare. This was the real thing.

She had to escape. She felt that she was suffocating. She had to get out at once.

All was blackness. Even the opening she had fallen through offered no light, only a less intense darkness. Could she climb up through it to freedom? But what could she use to make a ladder? Hay and gunnysacks?

The walls were closing in on her. The darkness

152

smothered her. In a terrified frenzy she started shrieking. She didn't know how loud or how long she screamed. Finally she dropped to the floor and her screams subsided into whimpers.

13

A Message in Purple

Janna quelled the urge to scream anymore. She must not lose control as she had done before. There was no one to help her. If she got out, it would be by her own ingenuity.

Janna groped her way around her prison: solid walls of rough-hewn wood as high as she could reach. There were no openings. This was the corn bin: It had to be tight enough to keep shelled corn from spilling out, so there wasn't a chance that she could find a hole large enough to climb through.

Perhaps she could dig out. But what with? The boards of the trapdoor that had fallen with her were rotten. Nevertheless, she scattered hay and gunnysacks as she scuffed her feet over every inch of the cement floor, hoping that somewhere she could find a break in the concrete. It was well-poured. Decades of use had neither cracked nor broken it.

The darkness oppressed her like a sack over her head. What if she was never found? Again and again she fought the unreasoning terror of claustrophobia. She could feel the dark walls compress silently around her, squeezing, smothering, stifling her in terrifying blackness. Again and again she forced down the urge to scream. If only she could see!

Janna sat down on the loose hay and took several

deep breaths. She compelled herself to think, to search with her mind for a way to escape. She knew her prison had an opening. But how could she reach upward through twelve feet of space? Could she possibly climb the walls of this room? Again she circled her dark dungeon, this time more slowly. Painstakingly she examined each board from floor level to as high as she could stretch. Cobwebs masked her face at one point and in panic she clawed them away. Her search revealed nothing except bare, rough walls.

In near despair Janna returned to the center of the room and sat on a pile of sacks and hay. The silence was broken by a tiny scurrying and scrambling somewhere around the walls. *Yuk! Mice.* She pulled up her knees and wrapped her arms around them to take up as little floor space as possible.

Think, Janna commanded her numb mind again.

And again she grappled with the problem. She couldn't walk out: The door was locked. She couldn't take it off its hinges because they were on the outside. She couldn't climb out. She couldn't dig out. Then her mind became hazy and she began to daydream. In her dream she saw the little room flooded with light, and she saw her dad beckoning to her from the other side of the open door. Laughing with joy, she floated from her prison into freedom. Janna slumped slowly into her pile of sacks and hay and slept.

Morning slipped silently into the dark bin. Thin fingers of light filtered through almost invisible cracks to bathe Janna's prison in soft gray dimness. Still she slept.

Early rising sparrows chirped and twittered as they flew in and out around the eaves of the barn. Two pigeons, perched on the topmost ridge, cooed monotonously.

Janna stirred. Still groggy with sleep, she stretched. Her bare arm touched cold concrete and she woke with a start. She shivered; then she lay still, eyes open but mind disoriented. Where was she? Why was she stiff and sore? Then she remembered.

She sat up with a shudder. But at least now she could see. See? No she couldn't—not that well, at least. Her glasses, could she find her glasses? She squinted at her dimly lit prison, confirming what her sightless search of the night before had told her: hay, gunnysacks, pieces of the trapdoor . . . and festooning cobwebs.

But where might her glasses be? She was almost afraid to look. Maybe contacts weren't such a bad idea, after all. She began to move about on all fours, gingerly pushing aside hay and lifting gunnysacks. There—in the fold of that gunnysack—nestled her glasses. She lifted them from their covering. She was amazed—and grateful. The lenses had picked up a few scratches, but they were secure in the frames and the frames were intact.

After reviewing her surroundings with 20/20 vision, she shifted her attention to what she could hear. Were there any sounds from the loft above? She listened. Only silence.

The light of day and newfound glasses caused optimism to rise. Maybe the door wasn't as secure as she thought. With sudden hope she scrambled to the door. She turned the metal handle and pushed. The door gave a fraction, but the lock on the other side held.

Janna returned to her pallet. She rubbed her sore

knee. What now? Perhaps the hired man would come. But not if he was a part of all this. She shivered.

She was so thirsty. Was Trebla already fixing breakfast? Was Trebla a part of this too? . . . No— no, her aunt couldn't be this wrong about her. . . . But when Janna didn't show up for breakfast, would Trebla care enough to search for her? Probably not. . . . But if Trebla heard her calling for help, surely she would respond. It was worth a try.

Janna went to the outside wall of the corn bin. She beat on it with her fists until her hands hurt. Then she screamed over and over, "Help! Trebla! Help!"

She pressed against the wall, waiting . . . listening . . . hoping. She heard only the fluttering and the cheeping of the sparrows in the eaves and the gnawing of a mouse as it ate a grain of corn.

Perhaps Trebla wasn't awake yet. At intervals Janna banged on the wall and screamed, but there was no response. It was as if she were alone in the world. A lump rose in her throat and her eyes misted.

She wondered what Mother and Dad were doing. Did Baby Lisa miss her? She should not have scolded Kerri for spilling the perfume she got on her last birthday. That seemed years ago. She hoped Claude had forgiven her for being too busy with a book when he had wanted her to play ball with him the day before she had left. She would give anything to be in Cincinnati with all of them right now. Would she ever see them again? It was almost as if they had died. She sobbed in self-pity. What if she starved to death here?

Janna shook her head. *Don't be silly! People don't starve to death quickly. Jesus went for forty days without food, and so have other people.*

Her stomach growled anyway. Surely Trebla was up by now. She'd try again to get her attention.

Janna beat on the wall until she feared she would break the bones in her hands. Then she screamed until she was hoarse. What more could she do? . . . She hadn't prayed yet. She bowed her head. "Lord, I'm in a mess. Please help me." Feeling better, Janna returned to the pile of hay she had slept on.

Ashamed that she hadn't thought of it earlier, she remembered Mother's cure-all for fear: Psalm 139. She quoted it softly to herself:

"You are all around me on every side. You protect me with your power.

"Where could I go to escape from You? Where could I get away from Your presence?

"If I went to heaven, You would be there. If I lay down in the world of the dead, You would be there.

"If I flew beyond the east or lived in the farthest place in the west,

"You would be there to lead me, You would be there to help me.

"Even darkness is not dark for You, and the night is as bright as day.

"Darkness and light are the same to You."

Of course the Lord was with her, even in this cramped, confining corn bin. But how could He get her out?

Janna had sat huddled in the corner for some time when she heard a faint sound that jerked her to a sitting position.

"Janna!" Someone was calling her name.

Then she remembered. This was Sunday! She was supposed to go with the Morrises to church. It was Mike! *Oh, God, don't let him leave without finding me,* she prayed. She dashed to the outside wall.

"I'm here!" she screamed. "I'm in the barn!" Then she beat on the wall with both fists. She stopped to listen. Nothing. Only the gossipy sparrows. Had Mike left? She screamed again and again. "Mike. I'm in the barn! Help!"

She stopped to listen. Then she heard his voice, closer now.

"Janna, where are you?"

"Mike! I'm here in the corn bin! Come let me out!"

Mike knocked out the makeshift peg that had been jammed in the metal half circle to hold the fastener in place. When the door swung open, Janna stumbled out. She threw her arms around him, and the vast relief she felt released the flood of tears she'd held back. He held her, patting her on the back like a baby. Finally she was quiet. She stepped back, suddenly shy, and brushed away the tears with the back of her hand. Her face was streaked with dirt.

Mike looked her over. "What happened? Who locked you in the corn bin?"

Quickly Janna told him about her night.

Mike's face grew serious. "You've got to leave this place. He could have killed you!"

Janna stared at him meekly. "I only meant to follow him, to find out where he came from. I didn't think about him catching me."

He shook his head. "He might have done lots worse than lock you in the corn bin." Noting the stunned expression on her face, he hesitated. Then he went on, but his voice was softer. "Until now, this 'cowboy' always ran from you. He's not running anymore, Janna. And we don't know how badly he wants what he's after."

Janna's raw nerves gave way. She turned her back

on Mike and burst into tears again. "I *had* to follow him," she wailed. "I *had* to try . . ."

Mike was instantly contrite. He turned her around and put his arms around her. She buried her face against his shoulder and sobbed for all of the fear and hurt of the night before.

"I'm sorry—I'm sorry." He patted her head. "I guess I'm treating you like one of the twins."

Finally Janna stepped back, red-eyed and sniffling. She managed a weak smile.

Mike's face was still serious. "That guy has to be caught. When we get to my house, my folks can go on to church, but we'll call the sheriff and meet him over here."

"Oh, Mike, I don't want to miss church. Not after this."

He looked at her with a puzzled expression.

"You made me realize how dangerous all this was. God protected me. I want to thank Him."

Mike's face slowly took on an amused expression as he eyed her appearance: Her face was streaked and smudged, pieces of hay stuck from her hair, her top featured a tear at one of the seams, and her hands and knees showed she had recently been on all fours.

"Well, it is still early," he said, looking at his watch. "My family won't be expecting us yet. . . . I'm glad I drove over here early to be sure you remembered. Sure, I guess we could all still get to church."

They had reached the house. "I'll hurry," promised Janna.

"I'm coming in," said Mike. "I want to be sure no one else is here."

"Oh!" said Janna. "I just thought of something: How are we going to get in the house? I think it's all locked up."

Mike smiled The Smile and headed for the tree at the corner of the house.

"But you'll mess up your clothes."

"That'll make two of us."

When he opened the back door, he said to her, "Look at your door."

At some time the day before, someone had installed a sliding lock at the top of her door where it wouldn't be noticed. Apparently after she had gone to sleep he had locked her in. The door was still bolted. Mike slipped the bolt, then turned the knob to open the door.

The room was just as she had left it. After Mike was satisfied, he left to examine the kitchen and the parlor. Then he stood guard in the hall.

Janna collected clean clothes, then dashed by him on her way to the kitchen. "I've always heard that cleanliness is next to godliness," she called back. "That must have been made up before indoor plumbing, because without it, cleanliness is about as hard to have as godliness."

She washed, brushed her hair, and put on clean clothes. As she hurried, she felt a thrill of happiness. She was no longer in danger, and Mike was worried about her! "Thank You, God, for answering my prayer," she said softly.

Janna was presentable when she emerged from the kitchen a few minutes later. "The kitchen doesn't seem to have been used this morning."

"Meow."

Janna jumped. "Oh, Prowler, you scared me!"

Mike laughed. "He came in when I stepped out on the front porch. He nosed at the kitchen door a couple of times while you were in there."

Prowler looked up at Janna with his big yellow eyes.

"Prowler, you're probably hungry—as a matter of fact, so am I—but I don't know if we have time to get you some food." As she said it, she looked at Mike, who was watching both of them.

Prowler's tail twitched back and forth rhythmically. "Meow," he repeated.

Mike grinned and nodded and they all headed for the kitchen. Janna knelt to pour food into Prowler's saucer. Then she stroked the back of the big gray cat. As she did so, she noticed a piece of yellowed newspaper folded in his collar. She pulled it out. In thick purple letters was one word: "Help."

Janna stared at the message.

"Mike, look!" She held out the scrap of paper.

He examined it, a puzzled look on his face. "You didn't write it?"

"No!" said Janna. "But I've seen that color before."

"So have I," said Mike.

She looked at him expectantly.

"It's called purple," he said with a straight face.

"Oooh!" she said, grabbing the piece of paper from him and staring at it. Her mind flashed an image of a spreading purple puddle on a white background. "Blackberry juice!" she exclaimed. "It looks like blackberry juice."

She ran to one of the kitchen shelves and located some jars of blackberries.

"Do you think whoever wrote that used one of them?" asked Mike as he watched Janna examine one of the jars.

"I don't know."

"As a matter of fact, he could have pulled a blackberry from a bush."

163

"Mike, you're supposed to be helping!"

Mike made a time-out gesture with his hands. "You're right . . . sorry. Uh, is that all the blackberries your aunt has? Does she have any more that she keeps someplace else?"

"I have an idea!" she exclaimed. "Come on!"

She was out the kitchen door and to the well house before Mike realized it.

"Mike, hurry. There's jars of blackberries on the bottom shelf in the cellar." She was waiting for Mike at the entrance to the well house.

Mike opened the door of the well house and stepped inside. "Well, they're not going anywhere," he said, facing the door to the cellar. It was closed and the heavy padlock was locked in place.

"The key's under the stove over here . . .," Janna's voice trailed off. "It's not here!"

For a moment Janna stood perplexed—then she dashed over to the cellar door and banged on it. Dropping to her knees, she shouted through the hole in the door, "Is anyone down there?" Turning her ear to the hole she waited.

A small, muffled voice rose from the cellar. "Yes! Help me!"

14

The Voice from the Cellar

So someone *was* trapped in the cellar.

Getting back to her feet, Janna remembered her own recent imprisonment and her anguished waiting for release. Every creeping moment had been torture. She stared at the cellar door. "How can we open it?"

Mike had been examining the lock. "It would take hours to saw through that heavy lock—even if we had a saw. But the hasp is held on by only two screws. If I had a screwdriver, I think I could get the door open by taking the hasp off the door frame."

"I know where there's one." Janna bounded back into the house. She had seen a large screwdriver when she had gotten the scissors from the kitchen.

Mike turned the first screw until it fell out. He was loosening the second screw in the hasp when Janna's old fears crowded out her empathy for whoever was calling out: How could they know who was in the cellar? Perhaps it was someone they would regret freeing.

"Wait, Mike. It could be a trap."

They heard the voice again. "Help!"

This time Mike dropped to his knees and shouted through the hole in the door. "Who is it?"

"It's me, Trebla."

Mike jumped to his feet. The second screw was out in no time. Using the screwdriver as a lever, he pried loose the hasp and opened the door. They clambered down the stairs. "We're coming."

"Janna, help me!" They could hear Trebla more clearly now. She was in the slatted wooden box at the far end of the cellar. On top of the box was the old egg crate. But it had been filled with jars of Aunt Agatha's preserves. More jars were stacked on top of the box, around the egg crate. On the concrete floor, here and there around the box, were broken jars of blueberries, beets, and green beans.

Mike and Janna began carefully putting the jars outside the egg crate back on the shelves. Then together they lifted off the egg crate and its contents. Soon Trebla pushed open the lid of the box. Stiffly she climbed out.

"Thanks. I wondered how long it would be 'til I was found." She stretched her arms as high as she could and lowered them. Then she bent from side to side and stretched out her legs. "Feels good to be able to straighten out."

"How long have you been in there?" asked Mike.

"What day is this?" Trebla asked.

"It's Sunday morning."

"Well, just since last night—but it feels lots longer," said Trebla, flexing her legs.

"Who did it?" asked Janna. "And why?" Finally she felt that some of the secrets were going to be solved!

"C'mon," said Trebla, heading for the steps. "I'll tell you when I'm out of here."

Janna and Mike followed Trebla out of the well house and into the kitchen. When she took an apple from the box, Janna followed suit. Then, following

Trebla's lead, they all trooped back outside again, where Trebla stood in the sun and concentrated on her apple.

Feeling a little foolish, as if he'd just finished a game of follow the leader, Mike said, "When I decided Janna wasn't in the house, I poked my head in the well house. I guess I didn't make very much noise though. Sorry."

Pausing over her apple, Trebla looked at Mike.

"I was trapped too," offered Janna.

"Last night?"

"Yes. . . . I woke up in the middle of the night and heard a noise upstairs. When I tried to get out of my room to see what it was, I couldn't. I was locked in. The screen on my window was the same way—but I cut the screen and got out onto the porch. I scared the guy out of the house by tossing some rocks at the upstairs front window where I saw his light. He came out on the roof of the back porch. He used that tree at the corner of the house for a ladder."

Janna laughed, reconstructing the scene. "But I guess about that time Prowler decided to do some singing—either that or they both spooked each other—because there was a yell and the guy jumped (or fell) out of the tree—it all happened so fast. He was almost to the barn when I saw him. I followed him, but he was waiting for me and we had a wrestling match. I guess he hurt his foot, because I accidently stepped on it and he let go of me. When he did that, I just ran.

"But instead of getting out of the barn, I was headed farther in. I wound up in the loft and fell through the trapdoor. Then he locked me in the corn bin."

"How did you get out?" asked Trebla.

"Mike found me this morning. Now, who locked *you* in the cellar?"

"I'd say the same guy." Trebla threw her apple core over the fence, in the direction of the big gray mare, who came to meet it. Trebla rubbed her hands on her jeans. "Peanut butter sandwich?" she asked as she headed once more for the kitchen. Janna had to bite her tongue to be patient. Mike looked at his watch. "We need to get going, Janna. Trebla, how about riding with us over to my place? I think my parents need to hear some of this. We can take you home from there, if you like."

As Mike got in the driver's seat, Trebla, peanut butter sandwich in hand, waved off Janna's invitation to follow her into the front seat. Instead, she slid into the middle of the back seat.

Immediately Janna turned to her, repeating herself, "Now who locked you in the cellar?"

A slight smile appeared on Trebla's face. She put her hand to her forehead. "Now who was that?"

Mike guffawed. It was the first sign of a sense of humor he had seen in Trebla.

"You guys!" cried Janna.

"Oh, I remember. The man who locked up both of us is someone my dad picked up." Trebla paused. "Have you heard that my dad has a drinking problem?"

Janna nodded.

"Well, Dad and this man—he calls him Slim—drank together a time or two and they got a mite too friendly."

"Has this guy been staying at your place?" asked Janna.

"He wanted to, but I talked my dad out of letting him. He was holed up in the cellar at the old Thomas place. (No one has lived there for years.) But he did use the barn loft to spy on the house and anybody who'd come up the road toward it. That's the main reason I tried to warn you away from it."

Janna shivered. "Why was Slim there?"

"Have you heard about the treasure hidden here?"

"Sure. But I don't believe it."

"Well, then, you don't believe your aunt. She told me herself. Slim believes it . . . and he wants it. Ever since Miss Agatha went to the hospital he's been lookin' for it."

"And you knew he was? Why did you let him?" Immediately Janna felt the old hostility rising between them. "I mean, I don't understand."

Trebla looked away, as if she were absorbed in the roadside scenery, and then said simply, "He said if he found it he'd give Miss Agatha most of it."

"But if there's a treasure, why doesn't she just get it herself?"

"She told me her husband hid it. So even she doesn't know where it is. Slim wanted to meet me after I visited with Miss Agatha yesterday and see if I had learned anything more about where the treasure might be. I told him I'd meet him at the well house about ten o'clock. I never even got into the house last night."

As Mike pulled into the driveway the twins burst out of the door. "What took you so long? We'll be late!"

"Wait till you hear," said Mike. "Even you two couldn't cook up anything this good!"

When they entered the living room they found Mike's parents waiting for them. But before any speeches of reprimand could be delivered, Mike said, "Janna and Trebla want to tell you something."

170

When the two girls had finished their accounts, Mr. Morris' face was grim. "I'm going to call the sheriff right now." After a brief conversation on the phone, he reported to the group, who had been listening, "We're to meet him at Miss Agatha's at 1:30." He looked at his watch. "We still have time to get to the worship service . . ."

Mrs. Morris spoke up. "Janna, I'm thankful that you're safe, but we can't let you stay at your aunt's place any longer. Sometime today we'll move you over . . . and Trebla, honey, you look tired. Would you like to stay here and take a nap?"

"Well, spending the night in a box did kind of wear me out, but I think I'll go home. But I'll be at Miss Agatha's place at 1:30. Maybe Dad can give me some idea of where Slim is, which the sheriff just might like to know."

"We'll drop you off on our way," said Mr. Morris.

Soon Janna was entering the small white country church with the Morris family.

She was so grateful to God for her release from the corn bin that every song and every prayer seemed to her to be a paean of praise. It seemed that even the minister's sermon was chosen for her. Its text was "I will never leave thee, nor forsake thee." After church, several people expressed concern about Aunt Agatha.

Janna ate with the Morrises and then dried dishes while Mrs. Morris washed them. The twins ran back and forth emptying the table, feeding scraps to Shep, the dog, and putting silverware in the drawer.

Watching the Morrises, Janna again wondered where Mike got his red hair and freckles and height. He didn't favor his short stocky father any more than he did his clear-complexioned mother. Perhaps Mike

171

was as different from his family as Janna was from hers.

When Janna had finished, she hung the tea towel on a rack near the sink. The atmosphere at the Morrises had been peaceful and homey, such a contrast to Briar Rose Manor.

Mike's dad entered the kitchen. "It's almost time to go."

"We're just finishing." Mrs. Morris let the dishwater out of the sink. The twins danced like dervishes around the table. Deidra stopped whirling. "This is the most exciting thing that's happened since . . ."

"Since Shep chased the skunk under the porch," finished Debra.

"Really?" Janna asked Mike.

He grinned and nodded. "I'll tell you about it sometime."

Trebla was on the front porch of the manor when they arrived. Janna noticed an old black bike, a girl's, lying in the front yard. Soon the sheriff and his deputy drove up and parked behind the Morrises' station wagon. Both men wore light blue uniforms, shiny badges, and guns. The sheriff was a middle-aged man with a round red face and receding blond hair. The deputy was younger and was bustling with importance.

The twins seemed awed by the two officers. Though they stayed close to their parents, they watched as the deputy examined and reexamined the lock over Janna's bedroom door and heard him say to Trebla as he once walked past her, "So you're the Wooten kid."

Trebla described Slim and told what she knew about him. She had learned from her father that he

172

was wanted for robbing a filling station. She told where he had been staying. The sheriff made notes as she talked. Then both Janna and Trebla told about Slim's search of the Mitchell house and about his treatment of them.

"You say you helped in the searching?" the sheriff asked Trebla.

Janna saw Trebla's body stiffen and the color drain from her face. She nodded, and then asked, "Am I in trouble?"

The sheriff seemed not to have heard the question, but the deputy spoke up, "If Miss Mitchell wants to press charges."

Soon after the sheriff and his deputy drove off, the Morrises, after reassurances, also left.

"I'm going to ride into Kay to see Aunt Agatha," said Janna. "I won't stay long. Why don't you come with me? That is your bike, isn't it?" She pointed toward the bicycle in the yard.

Trebla nodded and then said, "I don't think so. I gotta do some thinking." She sat down on the porch steps and watched as Janna got Mike's old bike from beside the house.

"Are you sure you won't go?"

"No, thanks. . . . Did you hear that deputy?"

"You mean the one that counted off steps between everything?"

Trebla gave a short laugh, but her face was soon serious again.

"I don't think you need to worry. Aunt Agatha would never press charges against you. . . . I hope you'll at least be here when I get back."

As she peddled toward the hospital, the burden of Aunt Agatha's tragedy descended again upon her. If she moved from the house, she felt her chances at saving the farm for her aunt would be lessened. She certainly wouldn't be able to find any treasure.

When Janna stood in the open door of room 202, she was relieved to see that her aunt seemed to be resting.

"Aunt Agatha," she said softly, taking a couple of steps into the room.

The woman's sunken brown eyes flickered, then opened drowsily. "Oh, Lucinda, I'm glad you've come."

Janna stopped suddenly and the smile left her face. Didn't Aunt Agatha remember her?

"You've been gone so long. Why were you gone so long?" Aunt Agatha's old voice was thin and petulant. Her bony fingers picked restlessly at the white blanket covering her. "You know we have to get the guest room ready. Bruce will arrive tomorrow." The querulous voice continued, "Did you get the blue muslin?"

Janna stared at the woman in consternation. She drew back like she had when she had found the dead baby rabbit. Almost as quickly, she was ashamed of her involuntary reaction.

She seated herself in the chair nearest the bed, then she reached out to place her hand comfortingly over her aunt's fidgety hand. Compassion flooded her heart. In one way, this old woman was a stranger to her, yet in still another way she was closer to Janna than anyone else on earth.

"It's all right," she told the woman. "I'll take care of everything."

As Janna left the room and turned into the corridor, she met a nurse. "What's wrong with my aunt?"

"She's disoriented. The thought of losing her home has upset her."

When Janna left the hospital her shoulders sagged.

Now what should she do? Aunt Agatha couldn't even advise her.

As she bicycled toward Briar Rose Manor, tears blinded her so that she could hardly see. She pulled off the road and sat slumped on the bank. Her heart was a lump of lead in her chest. She was alone. Completely alone. She belonged to no one and she had no one. Before, when she realized that the Edmundsons were not truly her family, she had had Aunt Agatha. Now even that comfort was gone.

A pickup whizzed by. Grass and weeds along the roadside waved in its wake.

"Hey," called a familiar voice. Janna looked up to see Mike coming toward her on his bike. "Is the bike giving you trouble?"

"No. . . . I've just come from the hospital." Janna's voice trembled as she looked into Mike's face. "Aunt Agatha didn't even know me. I came to be with her, and she doesn't even know me. I'm all alone."

Mike got off his bike and sat down beside her, shoulder to shoulder. He picked up some pebbles and began tossing them into the road one by one. Perched on a nearby weed, a small butterfly dried its wings in the summer sun.

Janna continued, "That's how I feel. Besides that, I don't know what to do next." She leaned her head on his shoulder.

Conscious of the weight on his shoulder, Mike merely fingered the pebble he had picked out of his other hand. "Before this happened, what were you planning to do?"

"Spend the night at your house. . . . Sort Aunt Agatha's things for the sale . . ."

"Well . . . if you didn't show up, it would sure disappoint the twins—and me."

She raised her head and returned his smile. Before she realized it, she had kissed him.

For a moment, neither one of them spoke, as they looked into each others' eyes. When it seemed she might fall into The Smile again, Janna jumped up. "I still need to do that—to sort Aunt Agatha's things. Now she needs me more than ever."

"Right," said Mike, still sitting and staring rather dreamily up at her.

"C'mon," said Janna, offering her hand. When he took it, she pulled him up and gave him a quick hug. "Thanks," she said softly.

Janna jumped on her bicycle and raced off, looking back for Mike to catch up. They raced until a hill slowed them. When Briar Rose Manor was in sight, Janna spoke: "I've got to get my things together, but it'll take the car. Do you want to wait, or go get it now?"

"I don't like to leave you but I'm on an errand, and I need to get home."

"Don't worry. I'll be fine. Besides, I think Trebla will be there."

"Well, why don't you head on over on the bike as soon as you're packed? Then we can come back together."

A few minutes later, as Janna leaned the bike against the front porch, she glanced around. Now that Mike was gone, she wasn't so sure that she was safe. However, there was no atmosphere of danger: Trebla's bike still lay in the yard. It could have been any quiet, peaceful Sunday afternoon in the country. Even so, Janna shivered as she slowly opened the front door.

15

Is Briar Rose Manor Lost?

"Trebla," she called, "are you here?"

"In the parlor."

Janna caught her breath when she saw Trebla. She was sitting on her cot—a violin in her lap.

Trebla looked at her quizzically.

An accusation started to form on Janna's lips, but she caught herself. "Right after I got here I was told that Aunt Agatha's husband played a violin and that sometimes his ghost was heard playing one. You may not believe me, but twice I've heard violin music and nobody was around."

Trebla smiled. "Well, that could've been me. Or Andy. Miss Agatha lets me and Andy use her violin anytime we want to. If Andy gets a notion, he's as like to play up in the barn loft as down in the cellar. He says it has a different sound wherever you play."

Janna laughed. "Really? You and Andy play the violin?"

"Miss Agatha taught me," Trebla said. "She used to be a violin teacher. I don't think her husband played though. Now Andy may of just picked it up. More than one person plays the fiddle around these parts."

"But why would either of you stop playing just when I heard you?"

"If it was me, I wasn't trying to scare you. And
could have, accidental like—or maybe *not* accidenta
like. He's as harmless as a moth, but he doesn't tak
to folks very fast. Maybe he was trying to spook yo
so you'd leave."

"Hmmmm," said Janna. "When I first came, h
warned me that there might be ghosts here. Mayb
then he was trying to scare me too."

Trebla got up from the cot and put the violin i
its case where it sat on the claw-footed table. "Ho
was Miss Agatha?"

"Oh, Trebla, it was awful." Tears glistened in Jan
na's eyes. "She didn't even know me. I didn't kno
what to do. She thought I was someone called Lu
cinda."

"I've seen her like that some. But she always come
around. It wouldn't surprise me if she was her ol
self by now."

"You really think so?"

"Yeah. You wanna go back and see?"

Janna welcomed the opportunity as well as th
company. "But if she does know us, let's not tell he
about last night . . . so she won't get worried."

"Good thinkin'. . . . But you look as if you'd had
good brawl." Trebla pointed to the bruises on Janna'
arms.

Janna inspected her left arm. It was circled with
a bracelet of black and blue finger marks. "Great—
it would be right at the wrist."

"Huh?"

"Well, it's just that I'm so tall it's hard to fin
something long-sleeved that will fit me. I'm always
having to leave the sleeves unbuttoned or push them
up. I've got a sweatshirt—but it's so hot!"

"Here. If you have to leave your sleeve unbuttoned

178

it might help." Trebla had taken off her watch with its wide leather band and was offering it to Janna.

Trebla continued, "I know it's not pretty, but my father gave it to me for my birthday. I don't think Aunt Agatha will notice today."

Trebla was surprised by Janna's sudden tearful hug, but said nothing.

At the hospital, Trebla leaned over the still, frail woman. She spoke quietly, and with such a tenderness that Janna was ashamed of herself for doubting Trebla's sincerity: "Miss Agatha, Janna and I have come to see you."

The sick woman looked blankly at her for a moment, then recognition flickered in her brown eyes. "Trebla?" she whispered.

Janna breathed a quick prayer of thanksgiving: Aunt Agatha was herself again. Janna watched as a gradual transformation occurred in her aunt. Alertness replaced the vagueness that had dimmed her eyes and slackened her face. She raised herself to a sitting position.

"She's okay now," Trebla whispered to Janna. She turned again to the woman on the bed.

"Miss Agatha, there have been lots of things going on this week that we haven't talked about because you were sick. We figure we can't wait any more."

Both Janna and her aunt waited as Trebla continued.

"I haven't been very nice to Janna. I'm sorry now. I wanted to make her leave and I thought I could do it by bein' mean to her." Trebla swallowed hard and Janna wondered if she was going to cry.

"Why on earth did you want her to leave? That doesn't sound like you."

"I thought I was helping you. I knew you needed

money, especially for the hospital and doctor bills
and I thought if the treasure could be found, it would
help. Slim said he would give you most of it if he
found it, or I'd never have let him look. But he couldn't
hunt as well with Janna there. So I wanted her to
go."

"Slim? Who is Slim?"

"Someone my dad met."

"But, Trebla, there *is* no treasure."

"I know you don't know where it is, but it's the
one your husband hid. You told me about it, remem
ber?"

Aunt Agatha was quiet for a moment. "There is
no treasure," she said softly. "I made up the story."

Trebla's eyes got big. "But why?"

Aunt Agatha looked at her hands clasped in her
lap. "I thought it was a harmless way to save my
pride. Maybe I should tell you and Janna about it . .
and hope you can understand and forgive an old
woman's deception."

Both girls waited as she organized her thoughts.

"I didn't marry until I was in my late forties. I had
resigned myself to living out my life alone when
Bruce came into my world. He was several years
younger than I and very handsome. It's hard for me
to say it, but I know now that he was interested in
me because I had inherited a fairly large sum of
money."

Janna was sitting on the edge of her chair, entranced by the woman's story.

"After our wedding he was away from home for
long periods of time. I circulated the story that he
was a prosperous businessman who was forced to
travel extensively. People seemed to believe me, and
my pride was protected."

Aunt Agatha paused and looked out the window. "Finally, after we'd been married about three years, he left me and I never saw him again. When he left, he took all my savings. After a time I took back my maiden name."

Janna's heart went out to her aunt, laid low with humiliation. She knew that she would never reveal her aunt's sad secret.

"But what about the hidden treasure story?" asked Trebla.

"Oh, yes—I got so caught up in my story I forgot that part. . . . Well, the neighbors could see that I was poverty-stricken—even though I had tried to make them believe that my husband was wealthy. I hinted that he had brought home a fortune but that he had died before telling me where he had hidden it. So you see, my dears, the hidden treasure is purely imaginary. Pride can inspire deceit, and mine did."

Janna patted her aunt's shoulder. "Don't worry about anything, Aunt Agatha. It doesn't make any difference; things are going to work out all right."

Aunt Agatha smiled bravely. "Of course they will, my dear. I'm only sorry that I *don't* have a treasure to share with you two. It's a sad thing to see Briar Rose Manor sold to strangers. I remember the stories my grandfather used to tell about the things he did there." She wiped her eyes with a handkerchief.

"Would you write down all those memories sometime, Aunt Agatha?" asked Janna.

Her aunt brightened. "I'd love to." She turned to Trebla. "Dear, while Janna's sorting and packing personal things, I'd appreciate it if you'd clean and polish the furniture. Perhaps that would make it sell better."

"Yes, ma'am." As Trebla spoke, a nurse appeared at the door with a tray of medicine.

"I'll have to ask you girls to leave," she said. "The doctor is requiring more rest for Miss Mitchell."

Both Janna and Trebla kissed Miss Agatha, then stepped out of the room.

Once outside the hospital, Janna took off Trebla's watch and handed it to her. "Thank you for the watch." Janna looked down. "Trebla . . . I want to apologize for the bad things I thought about you. And for throwing the dishcloth at you. Please forgive me."

Trebla laughed. "If you hadn't run out the door, I'd have scrubbed your face with it. But it's funny now. I'll forgive you if you'll forgive me."

Janna smiled. "I think I can do that."

As the girls peddled back toward Briar Rose Manor, Janna realized she was feeling the best she had felt since coming to Missouri. The mystery was beginning to be solved, she was on speaking terms with Trebla, and Aunt Agatha was getting better. But some questions still nagged at her.

"Do you know why the upstairs rooms were locked sometimes and then sometimes they weren't?"

"That was Slim's doings. He had a skeleton key that let him in all the rooms—"

"Skeleton key?"

"Yeah. That's a key that's been filed away in places so it can work on more locks. It's a kind of homemade master key for the older locks on homes like Miss Agatha's. . . . Anyway, Slim got a kick out of making you uneasy. He's a real weirdo. But I told him to stay out of Miss Agatha's room, that I'd been through it already. I didn't like the thought of him messing with her things. I'm not sure he stayed out, but if he didn't, he made sure he always left it locked!"

"Hmmm ... last night wasn't the first night I caught him in one of the rooms," said Janna, remembering with a shudder. "It's strange that he didn't lock the door before he began his search."

"Either he didn't think he'd wake you or he didn't think you'd be brave enough to walk in on him if he did."

From a field of corn came the cawing of a crow. Janna watched her front tire play tag with Trebla's shadow. She pushed her glasses up on her nose. "Why didn't your dad turn Slim in if he was wanted for robbery?"

"Dad and the law don't get along. He tries to stay clear of them."

"So that was part of the deputy's problem with you. . . . You said your father helped Slim. How?"

"You remember the night a ghost walked up the stairs?"

"Of course I remember!"

"That was Dad."

"Really? But then one night Andy was dressed like a ghost too. I followed him out of the barn lot one evening. At least I think it was Andy. I know it was his dog."

"Dad pulled that stunt just once—on the stairs. I'd say it was Andy you were following. He belongs to the Ku Klux Klan. They meet in a cave over in the valley. His wife is against the Klan and doesn't know he belongs. He always sheets up at Aunt Agatha's— in her barn—before he goes to a meeting."

Janna laughed. "He scared me too. . . . But if you and your dad were helping Slim search for the treasure, why did he lock you in the cellar?"

"Because I quit helping—last night. When I told him that Miss Agatha was going to have to sell the house, he said he'd have to find the hidden money fast while he still had the chance. And he said that meant getting rid of you."

Janna remembered the strong hands that had grabbed her in the barn and she shuddered.

Trebla continued. "I already felt bad about being so mean, but that scared me. I wasn't going to let him go any further. I told him that he'd be smart to just clear out, that if he didn't, he was askin' for a visit from the sheriff. That's when he grabbed me and dragged me to the cellar and pushed me into that box. I yelled, but there wasn't anyone to hear me—"

"But I did hear you," said Janna, and she almost came to a stop.

"Huh?" said Trebla, looking back and slowing.

"Oh, I'm so sorry. I thought I was dreaming."

Trebla shrugged. "Well, it's over anyway."

"Your note was written with blackberry juice, wasn't it? How did you do that?"

Trebla held up a stained forefinger and laughed. Janna peddled up beside her for a better look.

"Slim did me a favor by dropping some blackberries when he was using Miss Agatha's canning to weight down the lid on the box. There were newspapers in the bottom of the box, so I had paper. I just stuck my finger between the slats of the box."

A look of admiration came on Janna's face.

"But it was that collar on Prowler that gave me the idea," said Trebla, looking deliberately at Janna. "I heard him yowling and jingling up in the well house. (I figure he came through the window where the pane is out. I knew he could get through the hole

in the cellar door because I had seen him do it before.)
He wanted to be fed: He couldn't catch any dinner
with those bells. I called him and he came right down
to me. I stuffed the note in his collar and hoped it'd
be found before it fell off."

As Briar Rose Manor came into view, Janna said,
"It's great to be free . . . but what are we going to do
about keeping Briar Rose Manor from being sold? It
means so much to Aunt Agatha."

"I know."

The girls rode into the yard.

"How long have you known Aunt Agatha?" Janna
asked.

"Ever since I was a little kid. I ran away from
home a lot. One day I wound up right there." She
pointed to the steps leading into the kitchen. "I was
looking for a new home. I heard Miss Agatha was
rich, and I thought maybe she'd hire me for her
housekeeper." Trebla smiled at the thought. "I kept
house for my dad, so I thought I knew how."

"I bet Aunt Agatha was nice to you."

"Like a grandmother. I guess she felt sorry for me.
She made me a bread and butter and honey sandwich. Then she told me that she did her own house-
work because she was poor too. She told me to go
back home. But she said I could come see her anytime. I guess she was lonely too."

"And she even taught you to play the violin?"

"Yep. One day I heard her play. I'd heard fiddle
playin' before, but what she played—and the way
she played—I'd never heard anything so beautiful.
So when she asked if I'd like to learn, I was ready.
She's been real good to me." Trebla's face grew sad.
"I just wish she didn't have to move. I don't know
whether or not she can stand it."

"I'm going to stay near her, no matter what happens," said Janna.

Janna put down the kickstand on Mike's bike; Trebla dropped hers in the yard. They sat on the steps of the porch.

"There's something else I wanted to ask you. Do you know anything about Kiah? He wears a green cloak. One day I saw him slinking through the barn lot. Then another time I saw him digging a grave in the woods, and while he dug he was singing a crazy, tuneless song."

"Are you sure he was digging a grave?"

"It looked like it."

"He was probably digging for roots. He makes medicine out of all kinds of wild plants. Quite a few people around here do."

"Would he do anything to hurt Aunt Agatha?"

"Naw. He's strange, all right, but I don't think he'd ever hurt anyone."

"There's one more thing that has bothered me. . . . After the rabbit died, I buried it. But someone dug it up, cut off its ears, and sent them to me with a warning note."

Trebla looked shocked. "Ugh! It must have been Slim. He's the only one who'd do something like that. I wish Dad had never met him."

"Wow, I feel a lot better, getting some of these mysteries cleared up!"

"It's your turn now," said Trebla. "One evening I came in after you were already in your room and you were talkin'. I heard my name and I stopped to listen. I thought you were talking to someone about me. Then I realized you were praying."

"Yes?"

186

"Does that—Why do you do that when you're not in church?"

Janna thought for a moment. She shot a prayer toward heaven that she would say the right things.

"I've gone to church most of my life, but about a year ago I became a Christian," she said. "Then I realized the difference between going to church and being a Christian. For one thing, it's a relationship . . . like being in a family. So I started talking to God whenever I needed someone to talk to."

She pushed her glasses up on her nose. "I guess I should tell you why I was talking about you. I've begun to see how much God loves me and takes care of me. It makes me want to please Him, so I've been asking Him to help me get along with you, which He has. We're friends now, aren't we?"

Trebla was thoughtful. "I didn't know that's what it meant to be a Christian."

Janna thanked God for giving her the right words.

"Are you sleeping here tonight?" Trebla asked.

"I promised the Morrises I'd stay with them. I need to explain some things to them. Maybe I'll move back tomorrow."

"Well, then, I guess I'll be sleeping at home, but I'll be coming over to talk to Andy about taking that lock down from over your door, fixing the screen, and finishin' the job on that broken tree limb."

"I'm sorry about the screen," said Janna.

"Wasn't anybody's fault but Slim's."

After deciding against a total move to the Morrises, Janna packed a few of her things and peddled over to their house.

The Morris family asked all kinds of questions about the happenings at the Manor. Janna told them much of the story, but she said nothing of her conversation with her aunt.

The twins were sorry that the manor housed no ghosts. Mrs. Morris was glad that Janna was safe. And Mike was just glad Janna was there.

Janna had a great sense of relief. But she felt that her last hope was gone. The mysteries had been solved, but Briar Rose Manor was still to be sold. The day of the auction was only two nights and a day away.

16

Help from the Past

The next morning after the milk delivery had been made, Janna and Mike peddled to Briar Rose Manor. As they dropped the kickstands on their bikes, Trebla came out the front door.

"Hi! I'm glad you're okay," said Janna. "Did you see Slim?"

"I didn't—but the sheriff did!" said Trebla, smacking the porch post with her hand. "He won't be looking around here for any more treasure."

"He was picked up—oh, great! Oh, wow, I'm so glad. Mike, did you hear that?" She grabbed him by the shoulders and hugged him, knocking her glasses askew.

Mike grinned and nodded.

"Oh, boy, I feel a lot better knowing he's not prowling around," said Janna, straightening her glasses.

"You could move back now that he's gone," said Trebla.

Janna laughed with relief. "Yeah, I could, couldn't I?" She was looking around—at the upstairs window where she had tossed the pebbles, at the well house—as if this were her first time at Briar Rose Manor and it held nothing but delightful possibilities.

"I could help you," said Trebla.

Janna's attention came back to Trebla. "Help me?" She looked up into Trebla's face.

"Move," said Trebla.

"Oh"—and Janna realized she really had Trebla's friendship—"okay ... ummm," and she laughed, "I tell you what, I'll come back if I ... can make breakfast every other day."

Trebla smiled and nodded. "Deal."

"We could have eggs and toast," Janna said, "or blackberries on pancakes, or cold cereal and fresh fruit, or ..."

"Okay, okay," said Trebla, "so oatmeal's not your favorite breakfast." She laughed.

And Janna and Mike laughed with her.

Suddenly Janna stopped. "What's that banging!"

Mike stopped his laughing and cocked his head. The sound was coming from the back of the house.

Trebla's face grew serious. "I've been hearing noises like that all morning ... since Andy got here," and she laughed again, joined first by Mike and then by Janna.

Finally Janna said, "Well, we've got a lot to do today, and since Andy's already started, I guess we'd better get started too."

"What can I do?" asked Mike.

Janna looked around. "The lawn could be mowed and the roses could use some trimming ... but Trebla and Andy would know more about it than I do."

"Andy knows about the outside work and how to get it done. He's fixin' what Slim tore up or was the cause of gettin' tore up." She gestured toward the back of the house. "He can tell you where things are for taking care of the yard."

The three got busy and worked all morning. Mike worked outside, and Trebla and Janna worked inside. Janna pulled back the heavy drapes that hung over the windows. The light made the rooms look less oppressive and cold.

Just before noon, Janna stepped out on the back porch to survey the outside work. Across the barn lot, she noticed Andy on a bench in the shade of the barn, eating a sandwich. His dog sat on its haunches in front of him, eyeing him. He pulled something from his lunch sack and held it out to the dog, who took it with surprising gentleness, hobbled a short distance away, and then fell to eating.

Janna saw the patched screen on her bedroom window onto the porch. She noticed the tar on the tree where once a limb had been. She walked around to the front yard, smelling the freshly cut grass. She looked up at the big gray house. It no longer represented mystery and danger; now it held only memories of past generations, and of Aunt Agatha. An air of sadness had replaced the severity of the old house; it could never be home like the sprawling, friendly house in Cincinnati.

After Briar Rose Manor was sold, Janna wondered where she would live. Perhaps she'd rent a room from some family. She would live in the town wherever Aunt Agatha lived.

After a lunch of hotdogs and saurkraut, Mike helped Janna move the bed in her room so she could sweep out the dustballs. He looked at the small trunk as if he had never seen it before.

"What's in this?"

"Diaries and letters and pictures. I showed them to you the other day."

"Huh, I don't remember that. Are they old?"

"As old as the house, I'd say," said Janna. She

opened the lid. "Look at the dates on some of these." She handed him a packet of letters.

He leafed through the stack of envelopes, stopping now and then to examine one.

"Janna," called Trebla, "could you come here, in the parlor, for a minute?"

"Sure," answered Janna.

A few minutes later, when she returned to her room, Janna found that Mike had closed the trunk and was preparing to leave.

"I just thought of an errand," he said. "I'll be back in a little while."

As he headed for the front door and his bicycle, Janna thought for a moment and then went into the kitchen. She came out carrying something wrapped in waxed paper and headed for the back door. After pausing on the steps, she walked resolutely toward the barn.

Andy was applying oil to the buggy's leather upholstery. Janna hadn't noticed before how thin and old he looked. His faded blue overalls hung loosely on his frame and his wrinkled skin hung loosely on his face. Janna hadn't noticed before, either, that his shoulders were slightly stooped. The three-legged dog lay under the buggy, its mouth open, panting.

"Hi, Andy."

"Afternoon, Miss Janna."

"I wanted to tell you how thankful I am that you've been here through the years for Aunt Agatha."

"She's a mighty fine woman," said Andy, straightening up, like a soldier coming to attention. "Been mighty proud to serve her."

"I also wanted to thank you for your work today, repairing things and getting the buggy ready for sale."

"You're welcome, Miss Janna, you're welcome," he said, bowing slightly. He reflected a moment. "But I can't help thinking it's a mournful day, Miss Janna. And tomorrow will be a dark day for the Old Missus."

"I feel the same way, Andy. I'm sure Aunt Agatha thought Briar Rose Manor would be her home as long as she lived. Everything here is special to her and it's sad that we have to get it ready to be sold, maybe even to strangers . . . "

He wiped his eyes with the back of his hand. "Poor old Missus."

Janna felt tears forming in her own eyes, but she reached out and patted his arm, trying to hold her breath so it wouldn't catch audibly. Before she lost control, Janna spoke, "Here, Andy, I brought your dog—uh Mutt, isn't it?—a hot dog left over from our lunch."

Andy brightened. "Well, thank you, Miss. Mutt'll like this," he said, accepting the wrapped hot dog with both hands, as if it were a delicate prize. "He sure will. Thank you."

Janna smiled and turned back to the house. Her thoughts returned to the sorting that Aunt Agatha had asked her to do. She went upstairs to the store-room and began examining the stacks of magazines and newspapers. Hearing a knock at the front door, Janna wondered vaguely who it might be, then remembered the auctioneer had told her he would be by the day before the sale to check on things.

As Janna went downstairs she heard voices at the front door. Trebla was there, and Mike. With them was a man she'd never seen before. He was a well-dressed older man.

"Janna, this is Mr. Jones. He's a philatelist," Mike introduced him.

"A what?" asked Janna.

"A philatelist. A stamp collector."

"He's the banker . . . Miss Agatha's banker," said Trebla.

"I'm both a banker and a philatelist," Mr. Jones said with a smile.

Mike turned to Janna. "When I left I took one of your letters. I thought that the stamp on it might be valuable. I didn't want to get your hopes up and then have to disappoint you, but I wanted Mr. Jones to see it. He says that this particular stamp is worth a lot of money."

"Mike tells me you have other old letters," said Mr. Jones. "May I see them?"

"Of course," said Janna. The group, with a restrained excitement, walked down the hall to Janna's bedroom. Janna carefully lifted the trunk from the closet, trying to keep her hopes from rising too high. After setting the trunk on the bed and opening the lid, she took out the stacks of letters.

"There are over two hundred letters here," she said as she handed some to the banker.

Mr. Jones slipped off the faded lavender ribbon and flipped through the letters, examining each stamp. He gave a low whistle.

"I haven't seen so many rare stamps in a private collection in a long time. Some of the people who wrote these letters must have been world travelers. There are several rare foreign stamps in the lot." His cheeks had a spot of red on each.

"How much are they worth?" Janna asked.

"I'd have to check my catalogs to be sure, but they'd bring a good sum. Are they for sale?"

Her aunt had given them to her, but Janna wasn't

194

thinking of herself when she quickly answered, "Yes, they are!"

"I'd like them all."

Pushing her glasses up on her nose, Janna looked from Trebla to Mike and then at Mr. Jones. "Well— I don't know anything about collecting stamps, or what they're worth."

"Everyone around here knows Mr. Jones," said Mike. "He's fair. He won't cheat you."

"Thanks, Mike," Mr. Jones patted Mike's shoulder. "I'll give you a good price," he told Janna.

"Then I guess we'll sell them to you," Janna said. She looked at Mike gratefully. He answered with a grin.

"If it's all right with you, I'd like to take all the letters home with me. I'll figure the value of the stamps. I should be ready to make you an offer in a couple of hours."

After Mr. Jones left, Janna, Trebla, and Mike continued their work cleaning up the house and polishing the furniture. However, the possibility of receiving money for the stamps was so exciting that they couldn't keep their minds on their tasks.

Time seemed to drag. Janna decided to clean the picture frames in the parlor and in Aunt Agatha's bedroom while she waited. She dusted and wiped and polished as she listened for the sound of a returning car.

"Lord, help me to make the right decision," she prayed out loud. "Work things out Your way."

Just as she had finished the last picture and re-hung it, Mr. Jones' Mercedes stopped in front of the house. Her hands were cold and her heart pounded as she met him at the door.

"I've brought my checkbook," said the banker. The two red spots which still glowed on his cheeks contradicted his calm voice. "But you may want me to deposit this sum directly into an account."

"How much do you think the stamps are worth?" asked Janna excitedly.

Mr. Jones grinned as he slowly said, "I'll pay you one hundred and twenty thousand dollars for the lot."

Janna's mouth dropped open. She was speechless.

"One hundred and twenty thousand dollars!" exclaimed Trebla. "Miss Agatha'll be rich!"

17

Home, Sweet Home

Finding her voice, Janna asked Mr. Jones in, leading him to the parlor. Her head was light and she seemed to have trouble breathing.

Since Aunt Agatha had given her the trunks and the letters, she felt confident in making a decision on the sale of the letters. Mike had said Mr. Jones was a fair man.

"Well?" Mr. Jones asked. "Will you accept my offer?"

Janna nodded. "Yes, I will."

Trebla jumped, she was so excited. Mike and Janna and Mr. Jones laughed at her.

Then they watched as Mr. Jones got out his checkbook.

"Shall I make it out to you . . . or Agatha Mitchell?"

"Oh, oh—to Aunt Agatha—I mean, Agatha Mitchell!"

Mr. Jones laughed along with Mike and Trebla. "Tell you what. I'll make it out to both of you. You can take it to Miss Mitchell so she can see it and endorse it. Then you come to the bank and endorse it there and we'll deposit it in an account for her."

Janna liked the idea, and she was feeling more comfortable with Mr. Jones all the time. He signed it with a flourish, which made the diamond on his little finger send off bright sparkles of color, and handed the check to Janna.

"I'd like to keep the letters," Janna told him.

"I thought you would. However, very old stamps should not be removed from their envelopes. I brought other envelopes to exchange with the originals."

Janna hesitated. "I don't mind trading envelopes, but I'd like to copy the names and addresses that are written on the old ones. Could I keep them long enough to do that?"

"You may if you like. Or I could have my secretary run off copies of them with our copier."

"That would be perfect!" said Janna. "That way I'd have the dated postmarks, too. . . . Could we ride to town with you?"

"Of course."

"I'll see you later," said Mike. "I've got to check in at home." As he left, Mr. Jones picked up the black briefcase in which he carried the letters. Then he and the girls went out to his car.

Janna felt as if she were in a dream. Mr. Jones dropped them off at the hospital with the understanding that they would be by later to deposit the check and pick up photocopies of the envelopes from his secretary. Janna and Trebla ran into the hospital.

As they walked down the corridor toward Aunt Agatha's room, Janna said, "Pinch me. If I'm only dreaming I need to know it before I tell Aunt Agatha."

Trebla obliged.

"Ouch! Okay—I'm awake!"

Trebla grinned mischievously.

"But I still can hardly believe this is happening," continued Janna.

Aunt Agatha was sitting in a chair facing the door when the girls entered her room. She looked alert and happy to see them.

"Aunt Agatha, you'll never guess what wonderful thing has happened—You're rich!" said Janna. Trebla nodded.

The welcoming smile faded from the old woman's face; it was replaced by a gentleness tinged with sadness. "Of course I'm rich little Pollyanna. I'm rich to have you two. That's not the kind of richness that will keep Briar Rose Manor from being sold though. But I'm not going to grieve about that today."

"Briar Rose Manor won't have to be sold. You're rich—in dollars! It was the stamps on those old letters." Janna pulled the check from her pocket, unfolded it, and placed it in her aunt's hands. "We sold them!"

Aunt Agatha's eyes widened as she looked at the piece of paper in her hands. Slowly she looked up at the girls, then back at the check, and then at the girls again; her mouth moved but no words were coming out.

"You remember all those old letters you had in the little trunk?"

"Well, yes . . . of course."

"The stamps are valuable to collectors, and Mr. Jones bought them."

"For one hundred and twenty thousand dollars!" exclaimed Trebla. She had been standing first on one foot and then on the other.

"One hundred and twenty thousand dollars?" repeated Aunt Agatha, a hand going up to her face. "Why, I never thought . . ."

Words tumbled from the lips of both girls at once. Explanations. Plans.

The old woman listened quietly, her eyes glistening. Finally she said, "I guess I shouldn't be too surprised. Janna, you said that you were praying. So was I. I was praying that I would stay at Briar Rose Manor unless God had a special reason for wanting me in the nursing home. In that case I was willing to go. But I'm grateful beyond words to be able to stay in my home."

"You'll soon be back there, too," said Janna. "Briar Rose Manor will seem like home to me, too, when you're there. I'll stay with you, and I can go to school here, and—"

"My dear, weren't you happy with the Edmundsons? Weren't they good to you?" Aunt Agatha asked.

"Oh, they were the most wonderful parents in the world!" exclaimed Janna. Her eyes misted and a pang of longing pierced her heart. With determination she pushed it away. She knew that she would always remember those years with the Edmundsons as the most joyous period of her life, but she belonged with Aunt Agatha. Her thoughts were interrupted by a question from her aunt.

"Why do you want to leave them?"

"It isn't that I want to leave them. It's that you are my own blood relative and you need me."

"Janna, dear, I love you for being willing to take care of an old woman, but it would be best if you went home to your parents."

Janna stopped, surprised. She had assumed that it was simply a matter of settling her own mind. "But they aren't my parents." Janna's eyes filled with tears. She sat down on the bed, her head down. Her aunt reached over and patted her hand. Janna sniffed. Looking at her aunt, she said, "Lately I've been feeling like a nobody because I was adopted. I don't look or act like Kerri or Claude or Lisa. Since I'm so different, sometimes I've wondered if Dad and Mother really love me."

Handing Janna a tissue, Aunt Agatha said, "It seems to me that because they adopted you, you should be even more sure of their love. They must have wanted you very much."

"But adoption seems second-best."

"Did you know that God used the idea of adoption as one of the ways to show how much He loves us?"

Although Aunt Agatha was addressing Janna's question, she was aware of Trebla, who stood quietly by.

"As sinners, we were so different from His Son that you would think He would want nothing to do with us. But far from it. He wanted to make us a part of His family; He wanted us to call Him Father, Janna, dear. So He sent His Son to make it possible. When we believe in and accept Jesus' sacrifice for us, we become God's child . . . adopted—but His child, nevertheless. We read about that, honey, in the fourth chapter of Galatians."

Janna looked at her aunt thoughtfully. "I guess I hadn't thought much about being adopted by God."

"Well, honey, you're new in the faith, so you can't be expected to know everything. There's another verse you can think about. It's in the third chapter of First John: 'Behold, what manner of love the Father hath bestowed upon us, that we should be called the sons of God' (that includes daughters, too, Hon— you'll see that in the modern translations). And then you think about this: The Edmundsons' adoption of you is a blessing and an honor. Their love for you and your love for them is stronger than even blood ties. They've given so much of themselves to you that they are your *true* parents. You belong with them. And don't ever let that relationship make you feel inferior."

Janna smiled. Then she thought about Aunt Agatha, alone in the world, without her.

"But if I go back to Cincinnati, what about you? The doctor said that you can't live alone."

"I think Trebla and I can arrange something that's satisfactory to the doctor."

Trebla's eyes were glowing as Aunt Agatha reached to pat her hand. Janna silently surveyed the two. She could see that a strong love, as well as need, bound them together, just as she was bound to Mother, Dad, Kerri, Claude, and Lisa.

Sudden rapture, such as she had never known before, flooded her body. It was as if the world were ringed with glory, dazzled with ecstasy. She felt that she would burst with the wonder of it.

She bent to kiss Aunt Agatha.

"I'll go back to Cincinnati. I guess that's where my heart is, after all; that the Edmundson's really are my family. But I love both of you and I'd want to come back often to visit."

"We'll fix a room especially for you," said her aunt firmly. "Which one would you like?"

"Since Trebla will be there a lot more than I will, I think she should have first choice." She turned to Trebla. "Which room would you like?"

"I'd like one of the upstairs rooms. It doesn't matter which one. I've always dreamed of having an upstairs bedroom."

"My first choice would be the room that I've been using," said Janna.

"Then that's settled," said Aunt Agatha. "Oh, there are so many things we'll do. I feel much stronger

202

already. We need to get carpenters and plumbers and painters. We'll make Briar Rose Manor look the way it used to look—but first let me endorse this check!"

Janna smiled at the old woman's enthusiasm. She had never seen her look so good.

Trebla stood up. "There's so much to do that I think we'd better start."

"I'll call Colonel Clark," said Janna. "We need to tell him that there's not going to be an auction. I hope there's time for him to cancel it."

"Be sure to have him send a bill of some kind," said Aunt Agatha, handing Janna the check. "I'm grateful for all his work.... But most of all I'm thankful that there won't be a sale."

When Janna talked to the auctioneer he assured her that with a few radio announcements he could notify most of the prospective buyers that the auction had been cancelled. "Even if it does mean I won't handle a sale, I'm glad it's been called off," he said. "I hated to be the one to sell Miss Agatha's home out from under her."

Though the house was not to be sold after all, the two girls decided to finish the cleaning they had started.

They were working together in the library when Trebla noticed that Janna was standing, dustcloth idle in her hand, as she stared into space. Trebla looked at her with amusement.

"What are you smiling all to yourself about?"

Janna laughed and went back to taking out books and dusting off their covers.

"Was I smiling? I guess it's just because I'm so happy."

And why shouldn't I be? she thought. *My prayers for Aunt Agatha have been answered and I've found where I belong. God worked everything out in ways I never expected.*

The next week passed quickly. Janna visited Aunt Agatha in the hospital every morning. In the afternoons she spent time with Mike and Trebla. They went caving and found a tennis court and swimming pool where they spent a few afternoons.

Janna enjoyed every day, knowing that soon she would be on her way back to Cincinnati. But she made the most of her time with her new friends.

Janna's time in Missouri was drawing to a close. She began to think more often about her family back in Cincinnati. She stopped in the Kay variety store after one of her visits to Aunt Agatha and bought some postcards of the Ozarks to show her family. She bought each of them a gift: a carving of a hillbilly for Claude, a pull-toy for Lisa, a purse for Kerri, and a framed picture of the Ozark hills for her parents.

Her last visit to Aunt Agatha before she went home was a long one; they still had a lifetime of sharing left. Janna was glad that she planned to visit every summer. That way they wouldn't have quite so much catching up to do.

"The doctor is amazed at how well I'm doing," Aunt Agatha told her. "He said that I should be able to go home the first of next week."

"That's great," Janna said. She hugged her aunt. "Trebla will be a big help."

"She's a very capable young lady—just like you."

"This vacation turned out different than I expected," Janna said. "But it was a good one."

"It's been very nice to have you here, especially since you children discovered the key to helping me keep my house."

Janna leaned over and kissed the woman on her cheek.

"On your visit next summer, I should be able to greet you at the door of Briar Rose when you arrive . . . and maybe you'll have a personal escort from a certain young man in the neighborhood."

Janna blushed.

Early the next morning Janna made her rounds of Briar Rose Manor to say good-bye to things that had become special to her. She patted the horse and gave her an apple. She got two eggs from the hen-house; then she talked to old Andy.

"It's right good you came when you did," he said. "If you hadn't, the old Missus probably wouldn't have a home. Seein' as how I've got used to you, wish you could stay."

"I'll come back often," she said, smiling. "Take care of Aunt Agatha—and Mutt—while I'm gone."

He nodded vigorously.

Accompanied by Prowler, Janna strolled back to the house. Trebla met her at the door.

"I wondered where you were," Trebla said. "Morrises will soon be here to take you to the bus station. Let me put those eggs in the cellar while you finish packing."

"Thanks," said Janna. "It won't take long. I'm ready except for changing clothes. You're going with us to the bus station, aren't you?"

Trebla smiled. "Yes."

When the Morrises came, Mike was the first one out of the station wagon, followed by the twins.

"Hi," he said.

"I kind of like 'hey' better than 'hi' when you meet someone," Janna said.

Mike laughed. "Don't leave me confused!"

"Well, at least I like it better when *you* say it. It's more you than 'hi' is."

"I'll remember that next year when you come back. Let me take that." He grabbed a suitcase in each hand. "Whoa! I think I'll do this one at a time," he said, putting down one of them and heading for the door.

"Let us carry the little trunk," squealed one of the twins.

Each grabbed an end and they staggered down the path toward the car until Trebla commandeered one end and the twins doubled up on the other. Janna followed them.

Mike came back for the other suitcase.

"Wait a minute, Janna," he said.

Janna stopped. Mike pulled out a small box from his pocket.

The wrapping paper had tiny red rosebuds on it and the box was tied with a red bow. Inside it Janna found a heart-shaped locket nestled on a bed of cotton.

"Look inside," said Mike.

Inside the locket she found a small, oval-shaped white opal. The sun brought out flashes of brilliant red, blue, and green.

"Dad cuts and polishes them," Mike said. "He let me do this one for you. I hope you like it."

Janna's eyes were shining. "It's beautiful Mike. I love it even more because you did it for me. Thank you." She kissed him gently.

"I wish you had stayed with your aunt." Mike's voice was husky.

"I'll come back. I promise. And until I do, I'll write. Will you write me back?"

"You bet."

Mike's face was still flushed when they reached the car.

The twins twisted around in the front seat and, as if on cue, began chanting, "Bubba-loves-Janna, Bubba-loves-Janna."

Mike got even redder, but he was grinning.

"Hush, you two," said Mrs. Morris.

As they drove toward Mineville, Janna turned to look back. "A lot has happened since I first saw Briar Rose Manor. It doesn't even look like the same place."

"It will look even more different the next time you come," said Trebla.

When Janna bought her ticket and checked her luggage she felt almost irrepressible laughter bubbling up inside her. She was going home!

The bus was only half full so Janna was able to get a window seat on the side where her friends stood. She couldn't believe she'd made such good friends in such a short time. She looked forward to making them even better friends. She waved goodbye as the bus pulled out of the station, then she gave herself over to thoughts of Dad, Mother, and the children. Brooke would be glad she was going to stay in Cincinnati. And Janna had so much to tell her.

Excitement filled her chest with a buoyancy that made her feel that any minute she was likely to float out of her seat and go springing down the aisle in happy bounces. Her eyes were bright and her cheeks faintly flushed as she stared out the window. She could envision the reunion with her family. The bear hugs. The kisses. The clamor of voices.

Her impatience made her feel that the bus wasn't going fast enough. She had to fight the impulse to open the door, leap out, and run all the way to Cincinnati.

This time she *knew* that she was going home. This time she knew that she was going where she belonged.